SOUNDED FORTH THE TRUMPET

PURSUIT OF LEE FROM GETTYSBURG; A NOVEL OF THE CIVIL WAR

James A. Sagerholm

Portraits and Maps By David John Murphy

Copyright © 2021 by James A. Sagerholm.

All rights reserved. No part of this book may be used or reproduced in any manner whatsoever without prior written consent of the authors, except as provided by the United States of America copyright law.

Published by Best Seller Publishing®, St. Augustine, FL
Best Seller Publishing® is a registered trademark.
Printed in the United States of America.
ISBN: 978-1-956649-29-1

This publication is designed to provide accurate and authoritative information with regard to the subject matter covered. It is sold with the understanding that the publisher is not engaged in rendering legal, accounting, or other professional advice. If legal advice or other expert assistance is required, the services of a competent professional should be sought. The opinions expressed by the authors in this book are not endorsed by Best Seller Publishing® and are the sole responsibility of the author rendering the opinion.

For more information, please write:
Best Seller Publishing®
53 Marine Street
St. Augustine, FL 32084
or call 1 (626) 765-9750
Visit us online at: www.BestSellerPublishing.org

DEDICATED
TO
THE MEN AND WOMEN WHO SERVED
IN
THE AMERICAN CIVIL WAR

May their example of sacrifice
be an everlasting
inspiration to all future generations
of Americans.

The destruction of the enemy's forces must always be the dominant consideration in war.

—Clausewitz, *On War*

Table of Contents

INTRODUCTION ix
JULY 3, 1863 1
JULY 4, 1863 13
JULY 5, 1863 35
JULY 6, 1863 51
JULY 7, 1863 63
JULY 8, 1863 93
JULY 9, 1863 101
JULY 10, 1863 127
EPILOGUE 131
AUTHOR'S NOTES 133
POSTSCRIPT 135

INTRODUCTION

The shocking defeat of the Union Army of the Potomac at Chancellorsville under the command of Major General Joseph Hooker on May 3, 1863, led to two major events: the invasion of Pennsylvania by the Army of Northern Virginia on June 25, 1863, and the eventual dismissal of Hooker and his replacement by Major General George G. Meade on June 28, 1863.

It was the intention of Confederate General Robert E. Lee to use the rich farmlands of Pennsylvania to replenish his Army of Northern Virginia while sheltering the ravaged fields of Virginia from further destruction by Union soldiers, and eventually, to seek and to so utterly defeat the Army of the Potomac as to cause it to cease being a fighting force. In so doing, Lee hoped to break the will of the North while gaining the recognition of the Confederacy as a legitimate nation by France and Great Britain.

Before taking on the Army of the Potomac, Lee recognized the need to permit his army to recover from the rigorous campaigns recently fought in Virginia. His men lacked proper clothing, including shoes, and needed to enjoy a period of subsisting on the abundant farm produce found in Pennsylvania. He therefore had ordered his army to refrain from any encounters that might lead to a major battle until he ordered otherwise.

Unfortunately for Lee, his cavalry arm, commanded by the dashing and impetuous Major General J. E. B. Stuart, had been taken by Stuart on a long ride around the Army of the Potomac which, unknown to Lee, was rapidly marching north to interpose the army between the Confederate invaders and the nation's capital. Situated on the Maryland side of the Potomac River immediately across from Virginia, Washington, D. C., was in a vulnerable location, a fact of which President Lincoln was acutely aware.

Contrary to Lee's order, Heth's division of Lieutenant General Ambrose Powell Hill's corps, when confronted by the cavalry of Union Brigadier General John Buford on the road from Chambersburg to Gettysburg, attacked the dismounted Union troopers. Faced with stiff opposition from the troopers, Heth fed more regiments into the fight. The Battle of Gettysburg had begun.

The battle fought at Gettysburg during the first three days of July in 1863 left both the Confederate and the Union armies bloodied and exhausted. It was President Lincoln's ardent wish that Meade, having successfully stopped Lee's invasion, would take advantage of the situation to so thoroughly whip Lee and his army that the Confederacy would be forced to sue for peace.

Such was not to be, however. Meade was convinced that his army needed to regroup and regain strength before they could attempt such a daunting task. In addition, he had lost his most experienced corps commanders with the death of Reynolds and the severe wounding of Hancock and Sickles. And lastly, he had been in command less than a week. Thus, Meade did not pursue the retreating Confederates until it was too late to prevent their escape to Virginia.

Was Lincoln asking for the impossible? If Meade had promptly moved to prevent the Army of Northern Virginia from crossing the Potomac back into Virginia, what would have been the likely outcome? Could Lee's army have indeed been so crippled by an aggressive Army of the Potomac that the South would lose Richmond, and so lose and end the war?

Area encompassing the Gettysburg campaign.

©David John Murphy

JULY 3, 1863

It had been another day of vicious fighting, with the casualties on both sides climbing ever higher, as Lee's army had once again attacked the Union line deployed on the slight rise of ground known as Cemetery Ridge. Lee had sent 48 regiments comprising about 12,000 men in a charge across the fields that lay between the Confederates on Seminary Ridge and the Union line, a magnificent spectacle of war, the Rebels advancing with parade ground precision, drums beating and colors snapping in the breeze. About halfway across the ground dipped, the lead ranks disappearing from the view of the tensely waiting Federals. The tops of the colors remained visible, bobbing up and down in time with the rhythmic beat of the drums. Then up out of the dip appeared again the great mass of men, advancing inexorably, the drums growing louder and louder. Now the voices of the officers and the sergeants could be heard, keeping the ranks aligned.

Suddenly, the whole length of the Union line erupted, cannons hurling lethal blasts of canister and grape, as well as fused shells bursting overhead, ripping large holes in the ranks of the oncoming Southerners. Still, on they came, heads bent as if walking into a heavy wind. Pickett's division of Virginians obliqued to the left to concentrate their attack on a small grouping of trees where the low stone wall sheltering the waiting Yankees angled back a bit and then again headed along the ridge line. Thousands of rifled muskets added their deadly rain of minie balls to the continuing blast of cannons, and the Rebel ranks were now melting as hundreds fell with no one to replace them.

James A. Sagerholm

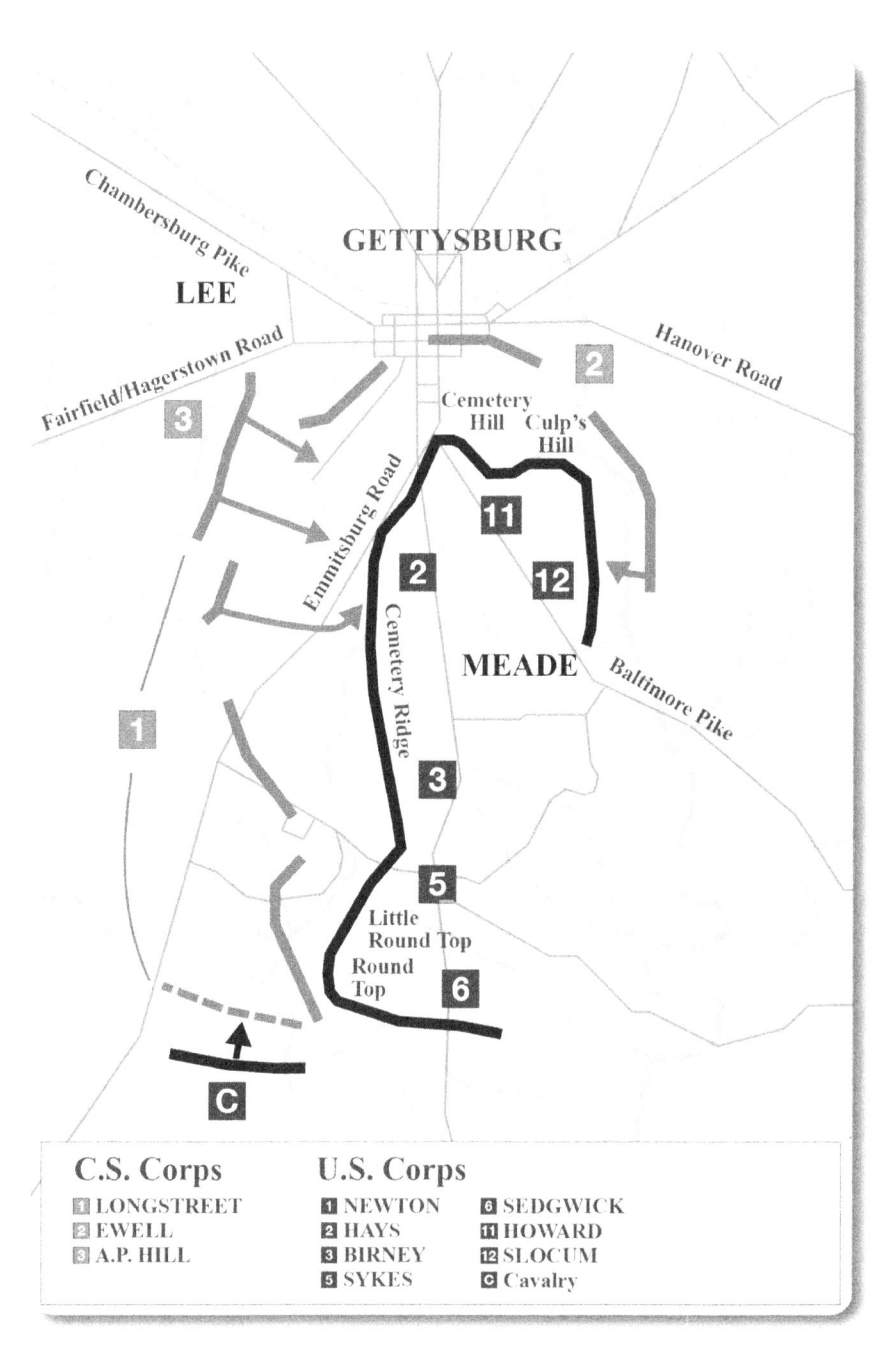

GETTYSBURG

LEE

Chambersburg Pike
Fairfield/Hagerstown Road
Hanover Road
Emmitsburg Road
Baltimore Pike

Cemetery Hill
Culp's Hill
Cemetery Ridge
MEADE
Little Round Top
Round Top

C.S. Corps
1. LONGSTREET
2. EWELL
3. A.P. HILL

U.S. Corps
1. NEWTON
2. HAYS
3. BIRNEY
5. SYKES
6. SEDGWICK
11. HOWARD
12. SLOCUM
C. Cavalry

Pickett's charge

©David John Murphy

Of the three brigade commanders in Pickett's division, only Lewis Armistead was still unhurt, leading his brigade on foot, sword raised with his hat atop it, guiding what was left of his brigade toward the cluster of trees. With a shout of triumph, Armistead and his now greatly reduced brigade leaped over the low stone wall, driving the Yankees back and taking possession of the gun whose crew had all been wounded or killed, the example of their young captain keeping them working their weapon until they were cut down by the Rebels. But Armistead and his men were now too few, and no reinforcements arrived. Armistead went down with a mortal wound, and minutes later it was over, the survivors of the charge streaming back to the Rebel line on Seminary Ridge.

The general commanding the charge was George Pickett, a Virginian, and it was his division of Virginians that had suffered the most casualties, more than the North Carolina regiments that had also participated in the charge. Lee saw Pickett returning and approached him.

"General Pickett, place your division in rear of this hill, and be ready to repel the advance of the enemy should they follow up their advantage."

Maj. Gen. George Pickett, CSA
David John Murphy

"General Lee, I have no division now. Armistead is down, Garnett is dead, and Kemper is mortally wounded," said Pickett, referring to his three brigade commanders.

Trying to rally the despondent Pickett, Lee said, "Come now, General Pickett, this has been my fight, and upon my shoulders rests the blame. The men and officers of your command have written the name of Virginia as high as it has ever been written before." Moreover, as Lee told Pickett, he considered that he himself was responsible for the failure of the charge, not Pickett.

Regardless of who was to blame, it was Pickett's duty to maintain the morale of his division. Instead, he succumbed to a condition of self-pity that clearly called for his being removed from command and sent to the rear. Lieutenant General Longstreet, commanding the First Corps to which

Pickett's division was attached, in fact so recommended, but Longstreet was from Georgia, and Pickett and his division were all Virginians. Lee could not bring himself to dismiss Pickett, for to do so would have been tacit admission of the failure of the sons of Virginia. Perhaps more importantly for Lee was that removing Pickett would appear as making Pickett a scapegoat for something which Lee rightly held to be his own responsibility.

Leaving Pickett to handle his personal demons, Lee and Longstreet quickly issued orders setting up a defensive line some hundred yards behind the original line occupied by the Confederate soldiers. Then they waited for the expected counterattack of the Union army.

* * *

Over on Cemetery Ridge, a courier from Meade's headquarters was informing the Union corps commanders to assemble immediately in the small cottage where Meade had set up his headquarters. In less than ten minutes, Major General Newton (First Corps), Brigadier General Hays (Second Corps), Major Generals Birney (Third Corps), Sykes (Fifth Corps), Sedgwick (Sixth Corps), Howard (Eleventh Corps) and Slocum (Twelfth Corps), had arrived and were seated while waiting for Meade to appear. There was no talking among them, each silently speculating whether General Meade would seize the moment, having twice now repulsed all that Lee had sent against Meade's army, for it was indeed Meade's army, and with that went the responsibility of deciding what that army would now do.

Major General Dan Butterfield, chief of the army's staff, entered, his right arm in a sling to ease the wound to his shoulder caused by a piece of shrapnel from a shell during the Confederate bombardment that had preceded Pickett's charge.

"General Meade will be here shortly," he announced.

Butterfield obviously was in pain, and Hays offered him his chair, which Butterfield gratefully slumped on to. As Meade entered, all except Butterfield stood and waited for their commander to speak.

"At ease, gentlemen. I have just completed a quick tour of our forces, and of the field. It appears that General Lee has pulled his lines back some and looks to be waiting for us to counterattack. But our men have been fully used up in repelling Lee's attacks yesterday and today, especially First,

Second and Third Corps. In my estimation, it would be foolhardy to order an attack at this time."

Meade meeting with his senior officers.
iStock.com

Meade had additional concerns that he could not discuss with his subordinate commanders. There was the loss of three veteran corps commanders, with Reynolds (First Corps) killed on July 1, Sickles (Third Corps) severely wounded on July 2, and Hancock (Second Corps) also wounded while directing the repulse of Pickett's charge that afternoon. Lastly, there was the nagging feeling of uncertainty borne of having been in command of the army just six days. True, his army had withstood Lee's attacks, but the thought of going over to the offensive and attacking the Army of Northern Virginia evoked memories of the defeats at Fredericksburg and Chancellorsville, memories not to be repeated.

Maj. Gen. George Meade, USA
©David John Murphy

A nodding of heads in agreement followed, but not all heads. Brigadier General Alexander Hays, commanding Second Corps in place of the wounded Hancock, spoke up.

"Sir, if I may, I bear an urgent message from General Hancock."

Meade nodded. "Please proceed."

"Thank you, sir. General Hancock sees this situation as an opportunity to deal a blow to the Army of Northern Virginia that could well result in ending the war. Several prisoners have separately informed us that Lee has only enough ammunition for one day's battle. Furthermore, the Rebels have so thoroughly scoured the farms, sending much if not most back to Virginia, they are now beginning to find it difficult to get enough food for the men and forage for the animals. With that in mind, General Hancock is advocating a close pursuit of the enemy who doubtless intends to return to Virginia as rapidly as his army can move. Recall that Lee left a pontoon bridge at Falling Waters." Pointing to a map of the area, Hays continued. "Here is Falling Waters, and ten miles north is Williamsport, where the Rebels crossed into Maryland. Williamsport has both a ford and a ferry—"

Hays was interrupted by a knock on the door, followed by the entrance of Major General Pleasonton, commander of the Cavalry Corps; Brigadier General Hunt, chief of artillery; and Brigadier General Benham, commanding the Engineer Brigade. Pleasonton spoke:

"Sorry to be late, General, I came as soon as Captain Meade found me, which was no easy task for him." Hunt and Benham echoed Pleasonton.

Meade was not given to being sentimental, but seeing his son in his dusty uniform, his face smudged with grime, brought memories of a boy being scolded by his mother for coming home from school with his clothes dusty and a tear in his shirt sleeve. How many mothers would never again see their sons? How much longer would this killing of Americans by Americans go on? How much more suffering must there be for the gods of war to be satisfied? Then his mind focused on Hays' words about possibly ending the war now. Now!

About this time, a breeze from the west came wafting across the battlefield and into the open windows and door of the cottage. While its cooling touch was welcome, the nauseating odor of death that it brought was not. Engineers, by the nature of their profession, tend to be practical and not given to the observance of ceremony or protocol, and Benham was no exception. He reached into an inner coat pocket, pulled out six cigars, and laying five of them on the table, lit up the sixth. The incense effect of the cigar smoke quickly enticed Sedgwick, Sykes, Newton and Birney to light up also, leaving the last cigar for Meade.

Butterfield had been Hooker's chief of staff, and working for Meade during the past six days, he had felt the wrath of Meade's explosive temper from time to time. He was thus surprised when Meade gestured for him to take the cigar, clearly out of sympathy for Butterfield's condition. Maybe Meade had a heart after all, he thought.

Meade turned to Hays who was patiently waiting. "Please continue, General."

"Thank you, sir. As I was saying, Williamsport has both a ford and a ferry. General Hancock recommends that General Pleasonton and his cavalry command be sent as soon as possible to Williamsport and Falling Waters to destroy the ferry at Williamsport and the pontoon bridge at Falling Waters. They should be prepared to hold Williamsport, if attacked, until the arrival of our infantry. The cavalry should also be alert to intercept any resupply of ammunition from Winchester. This latter task is of the utmost importance. If we fail to cut Lee's line of supply, defeating him becomes doubtful.

"In addition to the cavalry, at least one corps, two, if possible, should quick march to Westminster and board trains for rapid travel via Baltimore and Harpers Ferry to the area northwest of Martinsburg, across from Williamsport and Falling Waters, to set up a blocking force. As you can see here on the map, the bend in the river forms a small peninsula across from Williamsport where a line of fortifications across the neck can interdict the road to Winchester.

"At the same time, General Halleck in Washington should be requested to send all available troops here to replace our losses and reinforce the blocking force across the river.

"The overall objective is to trap Lee's army against the river and prevent his escape into Virginia. With him

Maj. Gen. W.S. Hancock, USA
©David John Murphy

surrounded, we do not have to attack, instead, we force him to surrender when food and ammunition are no longer available to him."

There was a knock on the door. It was Captain Lawrence, the staff communications officer. "General, I have a message from General French at Frederick, reporting that the river is rising fairly rapidly, due to heavy rainfall in the mountains west of here. He also reports that his cavalry has destroyed the Rebel pontoon bridge at Falling Waters."

Hays spoke up, excitement in his voice. "Sir, that will considerably aid us if we follow General Hancock's recommendations." Murmurs of agreement could be heard.

Glancing around the room, Meade saw excitement and approval among his corps commanders. Although he had lingering concerns, Meade was persuaded by Hancock's spirited message, and by the apparent agreement of his corps commanders.

"Gentlemen, I am approving General Hancock's recommendations. Let's get on with implementing them without delay."

* * *

Two hours had elapsed and other than some reconnaissance probes, there had been no signs of a Union counter-attack.

It was clear to Lee that he must now take his army back to Virginia. After three days of heavy combat, he estimated that he was down to about 35,000 effective troops, which was some 65% of the force with which he had invaded Pennsylvania. In addition, ammunition was sufficient for only one day of heavy combat. He had sent several couriers to Winchester with an urgent request for re-supply of ammunition, but it would take a day or so for the ammunition to reach the crossing at Williamsport, Maryland, the location where Lee intended to cross the Potomac River into Virginia. There was also the growing problem of food and forage.

Lee and Longstreet rode west on the Chambersburg pike to the tent where Lieutenant General A. P. Hill, commanding the Third Corps, had his headquarters. Lee thought it to be a more secure location for a meeting of the army's top commanders, better than his headquarters near the Lutheran Seminary that gave the name to the ridge occupied by his army. Hill greeted them as they arrived, followed shortly by the Second Corps commander, Lieutenant General Richard Ewell and Major General J. E. B. "Jeb" Stuart, commanding the cavalry. Major Walter Taylor, Lee's senior aide, slipped quietly into the tent and took position near Lee.

Lee stood up, erect as ever, but showing the weariness caused by the stress of the past three days and the lack of sleep.

"Gentlemen, I brought the army here to accomplish three objectives; first, to obtain badly needed provisions for our men; second, to bring the war and its effects to the people of the North while drawing the armies of the North out of Virginia; and third, at the appropriate time and place, to so badly whip the Army of the Potomac as to render it no longer capable of combat, thereby causing the North to sue for peace. I have failed to accomplish the third objective, and we must now return to Virginia."

Lt. Gen. James "Pete" Longstreet, CSA
©David John Murphy

Lt. Gen. Richard Ewell, CSA
©David John Murphy

Lt. Gen. A. P. Hill, CSA
©David John Murphy

Longstreet breathed a heavy sigh and nodded his head in agreement. A Georgian, he was the only one in the tent who was not a Virginian. Longstreet had disagreed with Lee's tactics at Gettysburg, advocating placing the Rebel army between Washington and the Union army, forcing the latter to attack instead of having the advantage of being defenders. Hill glanced at Longstreet, wondering if his demeanor implied a kind of "I told you so." But Lee showed no reaction and continued speaking.

"Before we can commence our departure, we must assume that Meade will try to press his advantage, so we must be ready to meet an attack. To that end, I have moved our line back to a stronger defensive position where even now the army is digging in. I have also ordered Second Corps to quietly withdraw from the Culp's Hill line and move into position to act as our reserve in the event that Meade attacks. If there is no attack, we will begin moving the army to Williamsport and Falling Waters where we will cross the river. Third Corps will move out first, with Second Corps filling in the line as Hill's men leave. First Corps will follow next, and then Second Corps, which will act as rear guard.

"We must also take back with us as many of our sick and wounded as possible, which requires obtaining as many covered wagons as can be found, this to be done immediately. General Imboden and his cavalry force will take the wagon train carrying the wounded across the mountain by way of Cashtown and then to Williamsport where he will cross into Virginia and continue to Winchester. Since the army will take the road to Fairfield, it will not be delayed by the wagons with the wounded. What remains of Pickett's division will be guarding the 4,000 Yankee prisoners, and will go with Imboden."

Lee turned toward Stuart who was standing next to Taylor. "General Stuart, it will be the task of the cavalry to protect our wagons from any attempts by the enemy cavalry to capture or destroy them, while also maintaining sufficient patrols to keep us informed of the enemy's movements."

Longstreet spoke up. "Sir, the countryside has been so thoroughly scoured, with all surpluses having been already sent to Winchester, we are facing a shortage of rations for our own men, and having 4,000 Yankees to feed makes the problem much worse. I propose that we parole the Yankees and leave them here for Meade to feed them." Longstreet said this knowing that one of his officers was already offering parole to any Yankees willing to sign the oath testifying to his word not to resume combat duty.

Lee responded. "I wish we could either make an exchange or offer parole, but when I suggested such to Meade under a flag of truce earlier, he informed me that he was unable to accept either suggestion due to orders from Stanton forbidding such. Knowing this, we should not offer parole when any man accepting it will face harsh punishment as a result."

Longstreet excused himself and left the tent. Calling his orderly who was nearby holding Longstreet's horse, he sent the orderly back with the order that all parole activity was to cease immediately. It would be up to Pickett to find food for the prisoners.

As Longstreet reentered the tent, Lee was speaking. "Tomorrow, we will remain here to await an attack from those people but be as ready as circumstances permit to commence our return to Virginia when ordered." With that, Lee dismissed his generals.

Longstreet was standing in front of the tent, undoing his horse's hitch from a tree limb. He was approached by Stuart.

"Pete, I'm glad you spoke up when you did. I was about to say something foolish about the need to protect Imboden's wagons when he has his own cavalry force whose men and mounts are in much better condition than my people. But while you were speaking, I had time to reconsider, and decided that it was wiser to just salute and go do as directed."

Longstreet was aware of Stuart's dislike for Imboden and was careful to remain neutral.

"Yep, it's going to be a rough go next week or so until we make it to Winchester. Of course, it all depends on what action Meade takes."

Sensing Longstreet's reluctance to discuss Imboden and his independent cavalry command, Stuart swung into the saddle of his horse, saluted, and rode off. Looking after him, Longstreet wondered why Stuart was so unfriendly to Imboden, and guessed it probably stemmed from resentment

Maj. Gen. J.E.B. Stuart, CSA
David John Murphy

over Imboden being independent of Stuart. He hoped it would not cause problems during what would be a very difficult retreat.

With that concern in mind, Longstreet handed his horse's reins to a passing soldier with the order to standby until he returned. He then went back into the tent for a talk with Lee about the protection of the wagons.

Lee was conferring with Hill concerning Hill's role as lead corps on the retreat, when he was interrupted by Longstreet's return.

"Yes, Pete?"

"General, Jeb just told me that his troopers and their mounts are not in good shape after the last week or so of hard riding and fighting. Imboden's people, on the other hand, are in good condition, and I recommend that the task of guarding the wagons be left to Imboden."

After a moment's pause, Lee nodded. "Thanks, I agree. I will have Taylor so inform them."

Longstreet departed, and Lee resumed his discussion with Hill.

JULY 4, 1863

Lee had remained with Hill after the meeting with his senior commanders, going over the details for the march back to Virginia in which the need for the lead corps to start promptly when ordered and march rapidly was critical to the success of the move. It was nearing one o'clock in the morning as a weary Traveler carried a weary Lee to his headquarters in a small stone house on the Chambersburg Pike, just west of the Lutheran seminary.

Near the stone house, Brigadier General J. D. Imboden rested under a tree, waiting for General Lee, having been told earlier that Lee wished to discuss Imboden's role in the retreat.

Imboden exercised independent command of 2100 cavalry troopers and had spent the time in Pennsylvania "procuring" sheep, cattle and grain as ordered by Lee, as well as whatever else his troopers deemed worth sending back to Virginia. So thorough had been their efforts that now it was becoming difficult to find food for the army and forage for the horses and mules.

Imboden had nodded into a light sleep, a sleep interrupted now by the clip-clop of a horse approaching. Standing up, he saw General Lee dismount with some difficulty. Lee stood with his arm across the saddle, his head resting on his arm. The moonlight set off the sculpture-like appearance of the motionless horse and Lee. After a minute or so, Imboden broke the silence.

"General, this has been a hard day on you."

Lee raised his head. "Yes, it has been a sad, sad day for us."

The silence continued for another minute, then Lee suddenly straightened, removing his arm from across the saddle, and turned to face Imboden.

"I never saw troops behave more magnificently than Pickett's division of Virginians did today in that grand charge upon the enemy," his voice trembling with emotion. After another minute or so, Lee bowed his head and, putting his right hand to his forehead, cried out "Too bad! Too bad! Oh! Too bad!"

Imboden had never seen Lee so emotional, but in a few minutes, Lee recovered, reverting to his usual dignified self.

Inviting Imboden inside, Lee recalled his brief discussion with Longstreet about Stuart. Sitting down at the table, Lee began his instructions to Imboden.

"We must now return to Virginia. As many of our poor wounded as possible must be taken home. I have sent for you to guard and conduct our wagons back to Virginia because your men and horses are fresh and in good condition. You will be faced with an arduous and dangerous task, for you will be harassed by the enemy's cavalry."

"Sir, my troops are all well mounted, including McClanahan's six-gun battery."

"I can spare you as much artillery as you may require," Lee offered, "but only one brigade of infantry. I shall need all I have to return by a different and shorter route than yours. Nearly all the transportation and the care of the wounded will be entrusted to you. You are to re-cross the mountain by the Chambersburg Road, and then proceed to Williamsport by any route you deem best. Do not halt until you reach the river. Rest there and feed your animals, then ford the river and do not halt again until you arrive at Winchester."

Lee then directed Imboden to collect as many wagons and ambulances as possible, and to be ready to move early in the morning. With that, Lee said good night, it now being close to two in the morning of the Fourth of July.

* * *

The 13th New Jersey was one of four regiments comprising the Third Brigade (Brigadier General Thomas Ruger, commanding), First Division, Twelfth Corps, occupying the extreme right of the Federal line defending

Culp's Hill, the rocky prominence that formed the northern flank of the Union army at Gettysburg.

Corporal Robert Barron had just relieved Sergeant Elijah Smith at the sentry post command shelter, sipping from a mug of thick black coffee when he became aware of the silence. The division of Rebels that had faced the Twelfth Corps for the past three days had been a noisy lot, whistling and yelling when dawn arrived and they were being rousted out of sleep. The glow in the eastern sky was growing steadily, but there was no noise, just the flickering fires outside the tents.

The 13th was stirring now, and Barron decided to inform his company commander, Captain Bumsted. Making his way among the grumbling, sleepy-eyed troops as they rolled up their blankets, Barron found Captain Bumsted as he was shaving.

"Captain, sir."

Bumsted, turning, "Yes, Corporal, what is it?"

"Sir, there is no noise coming from the Rebels. Their tents are still there, and their fires are still burning, but I don't think there is anyone there."

Bumsted put his razor in its case, wiped his face with a towel, and then, having realized the need to confirm Barron's conjecture, decided that he personally would lead a patrol to scout the Rebel line.

"Barron, I want a squad of ten men and you to accompany me on a reconnaissance of the Rebel line. Be ready in five minutes."

As Barron saluted and left, Bumsted put on his coat, and then strapped his Navy Colt side-arm around his waist, after first checking that it was fully loaded, and his cartridge case was full. At that moment, Sergeant Smith appeared to check on any orders for the day. Bumsted informed Smith about the patrol and asked him to tell 1st Lieutenant Roberts, adding that the company was to be ready for duty after a quick breakfast.

Barron appeared, reporting the squad was ready. He and Captain Bumsted shouldered through the troops who by now knew that something was afoot.

Bumsted led the patrol past the spring nearby, staying among the cover of some trees. Pausing, he uncased his field glasses and began scanning the Confederate line. Not a single soul was to be seen. He then scanned the area behind the line where he saw fires that were showing signs of flickering out amid some tents, but most telling of all, there were no stacked weapons anywhere.

"Corporal Barron!"

"Sir!"

"Go back and inform Colonel Carman that Ewell's lines are empty opposite Twelfth Corps. I will go on for a further scout of the area and will return within the hour to give him any further information. Quickly, Corporal!"

Barron moved out at a run, as Bumsted and the patrol broke out of the woods and headed toward the Rebel line.

Several minutes later, a winded Barron told the sentry outside Colonel Carman's tent that he needed to see the colonel without delay. The tent flap parted and Carman, who had heard Barron, came out.

"What is it, Corporal?"

Barron, as rapidly as he could speak while gasping for air, relayed Captain Bumsted's message to the colonel. Carman called for his horse and told Barron to mount up on one of the staff horses. Carman then led the way to General Williams' tent, where the commander of the First Division, Twelfth Corps, was having breakfast.

Surprised by the unexpected arrival of Colonel Carman and an infantry corporal riding what appeared to be an officer's horse, Williams jumped up as Carman slid off his mount, saluted, and told Williams of the apparent abandonment of the Rebel lines opposite Twelfth Corps, noting that due to the importance of the information, he had bypassed Brigadier General Ruger, his brigade commander.

Williams' adjutant had been breakfasting with the general and had heard Carman's report. Turning to him, Williams instructed him to inform General Slocum, adding that First Division was to be called to arms in anticipation of orders from General Meade to attack the Rebels who were apparently retreating.

Then, to Colonel Carman, "Have Captain Bumsted report to me with any additional information he may have."

As Carman and Barron rode back to the 13th New Jersey, it was evident that word of the Rebel retreat and the expectation of attacking Lee had swept through the regiments, where men were busily preparing for what many were hoping would be the destruction of Lee's army and the end of the war.

* * *

Walter Taylor gently nudged a sleeping Lee with one hand while holding a steaming mug of real coffee for Lee, thanks to the "generosity" of some citizens of Gettysburg.

As Lee roused out of his slumber, he glanced at his watch, noting the time at just 5:00 am. Taylor informed him that Second Corps had completed its move, and all corps were ready for the expected attack. He added that Imboden had started the evacuation of the wounded and sick in a train of well over a thousand wagons, a train that would stretch almost twenty miles from the lead wagon to the tail end.

The combination of good strong coffee and three hours of sleep made Lee feel much better than when he had retired. Now, if Meade would do what the armchair tacticians said he should and order his army to attack, Lee anticipated giving him a good drubbing that would even the account.

* * *

Meade had just returned from Culp's Hill where he and Slocum had discussed the meaning of Ewell's abandonment of the Culp's Hill line. Was it the beginning of the Rebel army's retreat or was Lee preparing to attack again, and if so, where? Although Meade was still firmly committed to Hancock's plan, he was not going to over-commit and let Lee turn the tables on him.

On entering the cottage being used as headquarters, Meade noticed that his chief of staff, Dan Butterfield, was sprawled in a chair, obviously in considerable pain. With all that was transpiring, it would not do to have Butterfield continue as chief of staff. Meade went over to him and gently touched him on his shoulder. Looking up, Butterfield tried to stand, but Meade shook his head, saying, "Dan, you are in no condition to continue on duty here. You need to be resting and under a doctor's care."

Turning, Meade stopped a young officer and told him to escort General Butterfield to the nearest medical site, and then find General Warren to inform him that he was now acting chief of staff.

There was also the need to fix his line of supply with Westminster, and with Ewell's withdrawal from the Hanover road, supply wagons could now accelerate the rate of resupply, bringing in badly needed shoes, clothing and food, as well as ammunition and forage. But it still would require several days to completely refill all needs. Could he wait that long and still be able to bag Lee?

Hancock had sent a note to Meade in which Hancock observed that the Rebel army was just as badly hit as was the Army of the Potomac, and if the Rebels could march, so could the Yankees, and if the Rebels could still fight so could the Yankees, and last, if the Rebels were motivated to fight by the desperate need to get back south, the Yankees should be motivated by the opportunity to whip Lee once and for all and so bring an end to the war.

After weighing all of these, Meade came to a decision and ordered all corps to be alert for another possible attack, with the most likely tactic being a flanking move around the southern end of the Union line that was anchored on the Round Tops. It would cut the route to Baltimore if successful. In the meantime, Meade and his staff, together with Brigadier General Herman Haupt, the officer charged with the responsibility of making the maximum effective use of the nation's railways, and a close friend of Meade going back to their cadet days at West Point, would wrestle with the question of the best location for the supply depot to support the Army of the Potomac in its effort to achieve the destruction of the Army of Northern Virginia. Meade had already decided that the Union army would move out as soon as the Rebels started their retreat, regardless of the condition of the troops. Haupt had commandeered every wagon possible, and a near constant stream of wagons was arriving, bearing the coveted shoes and clothing, mixed with wagons bringing bread, potatoes and beef, the latter from cattle butchered at Westminster, and loads of ammunition and powder.

The choices were either Westminster or Frederick, the former if Lee decided to stay in the mountains west of Gettysburg, and the latter if he went to Williamsport. The question could not be resolved until Lee's intentions became clear.

In Washington, Secretary of War Edwin Stanton, Secretary of the Navy Gideon Welles, and Major General Henry Halleck were meeting with President Lincoln to discuss Halleck's proposal. "Old Brains" Halleck, general-in-chief, had quickly recognized the opportunity for Meade to give Lee the final blow that would cause the Army of Northern Virginia to cease as a fighting entity.

In response to Meade's request for reinforcements, he had obtained Stanton's approval to bring the Ninth Corps, commanded by Major General J. G. Parke, from the Department of the Ohio, and had received word that the Ninth Corps was on its way by train, scheduled to arrive in Baltimore on the 6th of July, and arrive at the site across from Williamsport the next day, again traveling by train via Harper's Ferry and Martinsburg.

Now, based on the latest news from Grant, who had reported several days ago that Vicksburg should fall within the week, Halleck was proposing that one of the corps of the Army of the Tennessee be detached immediately following the capture of Vicksburg, to be transported by steamboat to Cincinnati, and then by rail to the blocking force, to add additional strength to it. In Halleck's mind, reducing the strength of Grant's army might also reduce the growing influence of Grant with Lincoln and Stanton, a reflection of the ill-feeling that existed between the two generals.

Lincoln studied the maps presented by Halleck, and raising his head, asked Halleck, "If Vicksburg fell tomorrow, when would the detached corps and General Grant arrive in Baltimore?"

Halleck replied, "It is about a four-day trip, three by steamboat and one by train, so they would arrive at Baltimore on the evening of the 8th or the morning of the 9th. It would be another day's journey to Martinsburg." Then Halleck looked at Lincoln, and asked, "Sir, did I understand you to include General Grant?"

"Yes, General, I want to get to know him better."

Halleck looked across the table to where Stanton was standing to see if the Secretary of War was as surprised as he was and was chagrined to note that the lack of reaction from Stanton indicated his prior knowledge and approval. Halleck's heart sank with the realization that Lincoln was bringing Grant from Vicksburg to supersede him as general-in-chief. Crestfallen, he stepped back from the table, his head bowed.

"Mister President," it was Welles speaking, "do I have your approval to alert Admiral Porter to have the necessary transports ready?"

"Yes, Mister Welles, you do. And Mr. Stanton, you may inform General Grant that I have approved General Halleck's timely proposal, for which I offer my sincere thanks to General Halleck. You may also inform him that you, General Halleck and I will meet him in Baltimore for an hour or so prior to his departure for Martinsburg. All of this should also be immediately sent to Meade for his information and planning. Please also tell Meade that I am immensely pleased about his decision to get Lee and that we will support him to the utmost."

* * *

Captain Bumsted and his squad had returned with two Rebel prisoners who had been found soundly asleep in one of the tents. They were both young and said they were glad to be out of the war now. Both were from a small town on the Eastern Shore of Maryland and asked if they could go home if they promised to stay out of the Confederate army. Corporal Barron asked their ages.

"I'm seventeen, and my cousin Jeff here is sixteen." Both looked at Barron with hopeful eyes.

"If we let you go, how would you be able to go home without a paper from your unit authorizing you to be away from your unit? You would be arrested as deserters."

The older lad spoke. "Corporal, you're forgettin' that we live in Maryland, which ain't a part of the Confederacy. Ain't nobody that can arrest us once we're home."

"By God, you're right," an embarrassed Barron admitted. "But if that's so, who enlisted you?"

Jeff said, "We ran off to Virginny, which ain't that far from where we live. We thought it would be fun to be sojers and whip ole Lincoln's boys. But it ain't that way."

Bumsted had been listening, and now entered the conversation. "What do you know of your army's plans?"

"Well, sir," Harry the older boy replied, "we were told that Gin'ral Lee is takin' the army back to Virginny. The wounded are goin' on a different road so as not to be in the way of the army. They had more wagons than ever I have seen, maybe a thousand. And we was told to be careful with our ammunition 'cause the army is runnin' short."

"Corporal, get these boys some food and a change of clothes, and I will ask General Ruger to let them go."

"Sir," said Harry, "I also heard that one of Stuart's men reported that the river is rising, and the ford at Williamsport is too deep to wade so they will have to use the ferry. Don't know if that is important."

Ruger sent Bumsted to Williams, who immediately sent one of his staff to Slocum with the information. Williams also approved releasing the boys and sent them each twenty dollars. He did not parole them in view of the order forbidding such but had them sign hand-written promises to never again serve the Southern cause.

Before releasing them, Barron sternly admonished them to avoid talking to anyone and to be careful with the money. They solemnly agreed and then shaking hands with Barron, started on the way to Baltimore. Barron watched them until they disappeared, thinking this had to be one of his better days in this war.

* * *

By early afternoon, a disappointed Lee, convinced that there would be no attack, ordered the retreat to commence at 5:00 pm, with Hill's corps leading the way down the Fairfield Road.

The rain had begun falling shortly before 5 pm, quickly becoming torrential, with strong gusts of wind that blew the rain into the eyes of both man and beast. The meadows overflowed, and streams that had been mere trickles became swift-flowing torrents that swept away fences and haystacks, strewing the debris across the roads. Nevertheless, Hill had his corps on the road to Fairfield at 5 pm sharp, the infantry of Anderson's division leading, followed by the division artillery and the accompanying wagon train carrying ammunition and the personal paraphernalia of the officers, as well as great piles of items taken from looted homes. Slave servants of various officers rode in the wagons to keep near their masters who mostly were on horseback.

Less than thirty minutes into the march, the artillery, the caissons, and the wagons began sinking into the mud that was churned by the feet of the infantry as the rain continued to deluge the hapless ill-clad soldiers. The result was at first a slowing of the column, quickly followed by a total stop as men and mules struggled to free the wheels of the heavy guns, caissons and wagons that were sinking down to the wheel hubs. Men were sinking up to their knees, and when they wrenched their legs and feet out of the muck, many began losing their shoes, sucked off their feet by the viscous mud. Two hours into the march, the head of the column had advanced less than two miles, with every step a struggle just to keep from falling as the mud and rain gave no mercy.

The officers who had horses found that riding on the grass-covered fields on either side of the road somewhat improved movement. The foot soldiers soon followed, as did the artillery and their wagons, but they still faced the formidable task of crossing the looming heights of South Mountain. The route chosen by Lee led his army through the narrow, winding Monterey Pass on a steep, stone-studded road that was difficult to traverse even in daylight, but they would be traveling in darkness and heavy rain, illuminated only by flashes of lightning, adding to the difficulty.

Route of Rebel retreat.
iStock.com

Hill's scouts had reported that the pass was free of any Yankee troops, but that was several hours ago, and for a moment, Hill felt a doubt and anxiety that he quickly dismissed. He had no choice but to push on, and if the Federals had somehow managed to place troops in the pass, it was his responsibility to sweep them out.

Anderson's division was in the lead. Daylight was waning as Hill and his cavalry escort found Anderson near the head of his column, urging the men to keep up the pace as they struggled against the wind, the driving sheets of rain, and the increasingly difficult condition of the terrain.

"General Anderson!"

"Sir," acknowledged Anderson, saluting.

"Have your lead brigade send forward a strong line of skirmishers when we reach the fork in the road that takes us over the mountain at Monterey Pass. We must be ready to take on any attempt by the Federals to block the pass."

"Yes, sir," replied Anderson, as Hill and his escorts swung their horses around and departed. At that moment, Major General Anderson was joined by Brigadier General Wilcox, whose brigade was at the head of the division. Wilcox had been alerted by a sergeant passing by that General Hill had been seen conferring with General Anderson.

After Anderson conveyed Hill's orders to Wilcox, the latter produced a map from his saddlebag, a map he had obtained from the talented cartographer, Major Jedediah Hotchkiss. Shielding the map with their hats, and after studying the map and the surrounding terrain features, Anderson and Wilcox agreed that it would be around 11 pm when they would reach the pass, provided that the troops could continue moving at their current pace. Seeing the unspoken question in Anderson's eyes, Wilcox shrugged, "We'll do the best we can, General. I can't promise more than that," he said as he rode off, head lowered against the wind and rain.

* * *

Lieutenant Alan Jordan, Signal Corps, Army of the Potomac, climbed to the top of the Adams County Courthouse, located near the center of Gettysburg. His watch showed the time to be nearing 4:30 pm. After the

Rebels cleared the town, the Eleventh and Twelfth Corps had moved in and now occupied the ravaged seat of Adams County. Looking down, Jordan saw blue-clad soldiers systematically searching house by house, street by street, and noted several gray and a few butternut uniforms among the blue, Rebel stragglers taken prisoner. Raising his field glasses, Jordan shifted his gaze toward the Confederate line now located several hundred yards behind the previous line on Seminary Ridge, extending north to Oak Ridge. Slowly scanning to his left, he stopped at the sight on the Chambersburg pike. Despite the heavy rain, he could see the road was filled with wagon after wagon, stretching down the road as far as could be seen and beyond, with more wagons arriving, coming down Herr Ridge Road and heading west onto the pike. Shifting his view farther left, he saw Fairfield Road where Confederate troops, whose regimental colors identified them as part of Hill's Third Corps, were beginning to fill the road, their columns facing toward Fairfield.

It was clear to Lieutenant Jordan that the Army of Northern Virginia was in full retreat and had no intention of attacking. It was also apparent to him that Lee had assumed a defensive posture with his new line which was well prepared to meet a Union attack.

Jordan scrambled down the stairs and ran to his horse. Within several minutes, he arrived at Meade's headquarters, where he found Meade and his staff working on plans for the pursuit of Lee as suggested by Hancock.

Meade looked up as Jordan entered. "Lieutenant?"

Jordan described the scene on Fairfield Road, together with as much of the details of the defensive line as he could discern and concluded with his opinion that the Rebels had no intention of attacking. In his excitement, he forgot to mention the long train of wagons heading west on the Chambersburg pike.

Turning to his acting chief of staff, Meade told Warren to look from the courthouse tower to see what his opinion was and to do so as quickly as possible. He then told Jordan to find Generals Howard, Sedgwick, Sykes, Pleasonton and Hays, repeating his information to each and then informing each to proceed to Meade's headquarters without delay. If Jordan was correct in his assessment, it was time to get the Union plan in action.

Sixth Corps being closest to Meade's headquarters, Jordan rode there first, where he found General Sedgwick conferring with his division commanders and his staff. Sykes also was present.

"General Sedgwick, sir, if I may interrupt."

Sensing Jordan's urgency, Sedgwick nodded.

"Sir, the Rebel army is in full retreat, and General Meade requests that you and General Sykes meet with him immediately at his headquarters." Saluting, Jordan mounted and rode off to find Pleasonton, Hays and Howard.

Sedgwick normally was not one who let himself be hurried, but his speed of departure this time surprised and so delighted his staff that several of the more junior officers let out whoops and were clapping their hands. when they realized the division commanders were frowning in disapproval. Then one of the generals, with a grin breaking out, raised his arm and shouted, "Up and at 'em! It looks like we're gonna get that old fox, Lee, once and for all!" The cheering started again, with the generals joining in.

Arriving at the headquarters that was bustling with activity, Sedgwick and Sykes entered the crowded cottage. Meade took the dripping wet pair over to the map on the wall where they were joined by Warren, who confirmed that the retreat had begun, and said it appeared from the regimental flags he had been able to identify that Hill's corps was in the lead, and Longstreet and Ewell were manning the defense line that Lee had set up. Warren also mentioned seeing the endless line of wagons heading west on the Chambersburg pike.

Pointing to the map, Meade touched the Fairfield Road, explaining that it was the road on which Hill's corps was marching. He then pointed to the Emmitsburg Road.

"As you can see, the Emmitsburg Road roughly parallels the Fairfield Road, and is west of the Baltimore pike. I want your corps to get on the Emmitsburg Road just as soon as you can do so, remaining even with Hill, to provide a blocking force in case Hill turns east to threaten Washington

Maj. Gen. John Sedgwick, USA
©David John Murphy

or Baltimore. If he should do so, engage him and inform me immediately. Sykes and his Fifth Corps will be following and is to support Sixth Corps if an engagement occurs. If Hill does not turn but continues through Fairfield, he likely will take the fork here that is the road to Monterey Pass over South Mountain, that being the shortest route to Hagerstown, and then to Williamsport.

"One of my staff who is familiar with this area told me that the road over Monterey Pass is narrow, winding, and has a number of large sharp rocks embedded in it. It will be dark when Hill reaches there, and the rain shows no sign of slackening, so if he pushes on, it will be a difficult passage in this weather on such a road, and should cause a significant slowing of his corps. Once you have determined that he will cross the mountain at Monterey Pass, your corps are to continue at best pace possible to Boonsboro, with Sykes continuing to Sharpsburg. This is to keep Lee from trying to threaten Washington or Baltimore. If there is a ferry at Sharpsburg, destroy it. Keep me informed as to where you are and what is happening."

Sedgwick and Sykes studied the map for a minute or so, then nodded, saluted and hurried out. Several minutes later, Sedgwick arrived at his tent, while Sykes hurried on to his corps. Sedgwick was greeted by an excited group waiting anxiously for the news from headquarters. Calling for paper and pencil, he then made a rough sketch from memory of the roads and locations of the towns that pertained to their tasking from Meade.

Straightening up from the table, he relayed the orders given him by Meade. Then he said, "Sixth Corps will do its duty and more if necessary, and we will help to take Bobby Lee down, or go down ourselves, but no one will be able to accuse Sixth Corps of not giving all we have and then some!"

Cheers erupted, followed by the rapid departure of the division commanders as the staff began assembling their things for the march.

Back at Meade's headquarters, Howard and Hays arrived from their respective corps almost at the same time. They entered the busy room and pushed their way to Meade, who was studying the map on the wall.

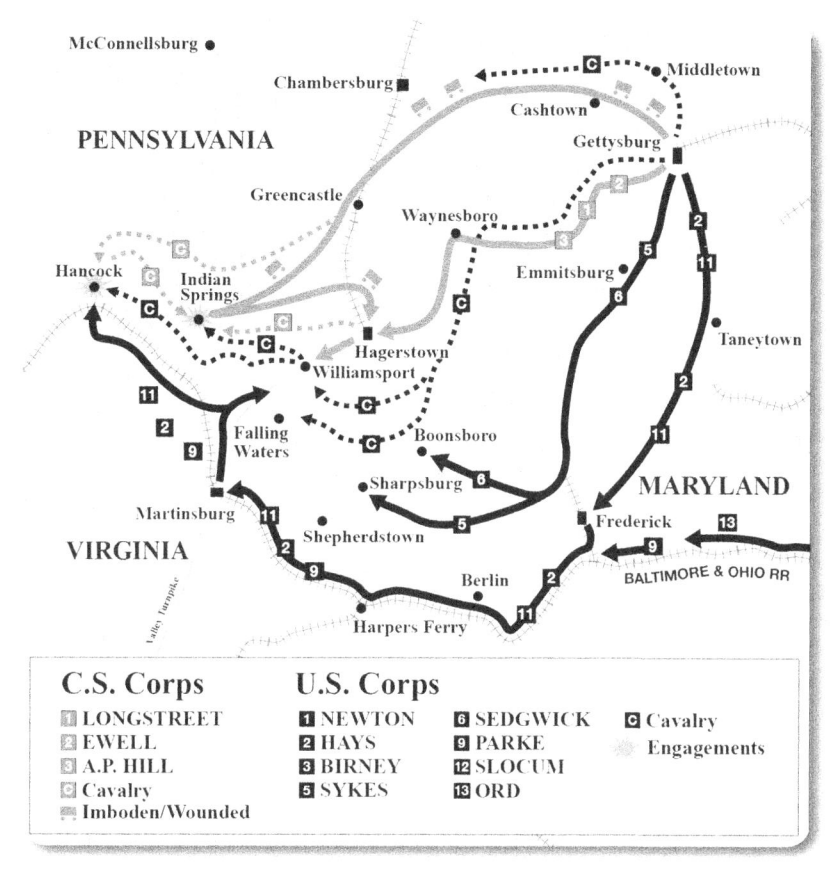

Retreat and pursuit.
©David John Murphy

C.S. Corps
1. LONGSTREET
2. EWELL
3. A.P. HILL
C. Cavalry
— Imboden/Wounded

U.S. Corps
1. NEWTON
2. HAYS
3. BIRNEY
5. SYKES
6. SEDGWICK
9. PARKE
12. SLOCUM
13. ORD
C. Cavalry
Engagements

Without preamble or greeting, Meade began speaking. "General Howard, I am convinced that Lee intends to cross into Virginia at Williamsport, since that will put him immediately on the Valley turnpike that leads directly to Winchester. Reports from General French affirm that his cavalry has destroyed Lee's pontoon bridge at Falling Waters, his alternate crossing point. French also reports that the river is rapidly rising and is expected to reach flood level this evening, leaving only the ferry at Williamsport as a means of crossing there. I have asked Pleasonton to have his cavalry destroy the ferry at Williamsport and any other ferries between Williamsport and the bridge at Hancock northwest of Williamsport. Sedgwick and Sykes are going to take blocking positions at Boonsboro and Sharpsburg."

Pointing to the river at Williamsport, Meade continued, "Note how the curve of the river here forms a small peninsula, with the Valley turnpike passing down the middle. Halleck has informed me that he has ordered the Ninth Corps to come east by train to block the Virginia side with a line across the base of that peninsula. They should arrive in about two days. He has also told Grant that, as soon as Vicksburg falls, which should be any day now, he is to send one of his corps by boat to Cincinnati, and then by train to Baltimore, Harpers Ferry and on up to Martinsburg to reinforce Howard. That is a three or four-day trip.

"In the meantime, your two corps will entrain at Hanover, and follow the same rail route to the Virginia side across from Williamsport. We will take advantage of the high water to set up an initial blocking force across the river opposite Williamsport. We know that Lee is short on ammunition, and no doubt has asked for resupply from Winchester. We must do all possible to prevent that. Except for Kilpatrick, Pleasonton and his cavalry are on the way to Williamsport which they will occupy until ordered elsewhere. Haupt has trains waiting at Hanover for your trip to Martinsburg, crossing at Harpers Ferry. The wagons bringing in supplies from Westminster will carry your troops to Hanover and then return to Westminster. Move out as soon as you are ready. General Howard, you will have overall command."

As they were leaving, Howard told Hays to have his corps at the wagon unloading area within the hour, and he would do the same. Hancock's plan, that had now evolved into Meade's plan, was quickly being implemented.

* * *

Wilcox and Anderson had done all they could to keep the division moving, but it was almost midnight when the weary Confederates at the head of the column stopped at the spot where a fork to the right started the ascent to Monterey Pass.

Anderson came riding out of the rear of the division where he was once again telling the file closers at the end of the division to be alert for stragglers and keep them moving with the division.

Wilcox had shaken out a company as skirmishers and so informed Anderson. It was about 11:30 pm, a half hour later than planned, but considering the conditions – pitch black night, strong winds that drove stinging sheets of cold, heavy rain, flooded streams, knee-deep mud on the road – the division had done well. But it was not without cost.

The combination of the black night and driving rain made it extremely difficult for the wagon teamsters to see the road, and at a sharp curve to the right, the lead wagon failed to see the curve and went straight over the side and down into the deep ravine below. The noise of the crashing wagon was lost in the howling wind and rain, and the next three wagons also went over the cliff, each smashing on top of the wagon ahead. The last seven wagons were saved when a bolt of lightning illuminated the road in time for the fifth wagon to see the curve, and the fourth wagon disappearing over the cliff. Lost with the wagons were the division records and half of the artillery rounds.

The storm gave no sign of weakening, yet men were so tired many fell asleep, standing in the cold, driving rain. As Wilcox was about to order the division forward and up the fork leading to the pass, Anderson said, "Wait."

He had noticed the condition of the men, and he was also aware that a hotel was nearby. If the Yankees had secured the pass, he doubted that his weary troops could be effective enough to drive them off. And maybe the hotel could be persuaded to have his division as guests for dinner. With a couple hours of rest and food in their bellies, they could hit the pass just before dawn and be in much better shape for the day's march. He told Wilcox what he had in mind and rode off to get Hill's approval.

* * *

Sedgwick was concerned. The corps had not marched as speedily as he intended, and he was worried that Hill would be well ahead of Sixth Corps. If so, Hill could turn toward Washington and prevent him and Sykes from blocking the Rebel army if Lee chose to attack the Union capital. Although it was nearing midnight, he and Sykes decided to keep moving until they reached Boonsboro. Once there, half of the troops could rest for an hour while the other half began digging in; at the end of the hour, they would shift. And if they found Hill had outmarched them, what then?

* * *

Pleasonton and the cavalry had ridden nine straight hours at a steady trot, resting for a half-hour every three hours. It was about 11:30 pm, and Pleasonton was mentally debating whether to rest for two more hours or rouse the troops and continue. In the rain and darkness, they had not so far encountered any of Stuart's troopers. But if they stayed at their present location, just outside of Middletown, they would be traveling in daylight, dawn being shortly after 4 am. With that in mind, he decided to keep moving, and sent couriers to the brigade commanders to form up and move out. With any luck, they should ride into Williamsport about an hour before dawn.

* * *

Lee could not sleep in the bouncing wagon and lay there considering his options and the options of his opponent. If the way was open, he could turn and threaten Baltimore or Washington or both. Tempting as that prospect was, he knew the prudent course was to return to Virginia, given the condition of his army. Besides, he had thousands of head of cattle and sheep that were needed in Virginia, especially Richmond, where the women were protesting the lack of food for their families.

He next reviewed in his mind the options that were available to Meade. Lee viewed Meade as being a competent corps commander, but did not think him sufficiently aggressive to take chances, so what was he likely to do with the added responsibility of army command? As he was pondering Meade's probable moves, he felt the wagon stop. It was Stuart who climbed up onto the seat facing Lee, who sat up as the wagon again moved on.

"General Lee, sorry to disturb you."

"What is it, General?"

"Sir, one of my troopers earlier tonight stopped at a farmhouse to get some food, and while he was there, the farmer commented that he had also fed some Yankee troopers. One of the Yanks asked the other about the time, and then figured they would be at Williamsport before dawn. My trooper immediately left and reported to Fitz who then informed me. I sent out patrols to find out where the Yanks were and in what force. One patrol spotted what looked like the entire cavalry of their army, just outside of Middletown.

At the same time, another patrol saw a large body of Federal infantry passing through Mechanicstown, my guess being they are headed to the Sharpsburg area."

Lee had a mental image of the map he had studied, and now he saw what he considered to be Meade's intention. With the river unfordable, Lee would have to use the ferry at Williamsport, so the Union cavalry were no doubt aiming to destroy the ferry while the Union infantry would prevent crossing lower down the river at Falling Waters, where he had left the pontoon bridge. The cavalry in Williamsport would also be in position to intercept the resupply of ammunition from Winchester. Imboden had mentioned that there were several ferries between Williamsport and Hancock, and that there was a stone bridge at Hancock. Imboden!

"General, please inform General Imboden to avoid Williamsport and why, and tell him I wish him to cross at the bridge at Hancock.

"The Union cavalry report is a matter of deep concern. You must get one of your brigades to Williamsport as quickly as possible. We must protect our logistics support from Winchester. With only enough ammunition for one day of combat, we need that resupply I have asked for. With the river flooding, the ferry at Williamsport is our only means of getting it across here. If we lose the ferry, the bridge at Hancock assumes vital importance. Send Fitz Lee to Hancock now and impress upon him the critical significance of controlling that bridge. If you must engage Pleasonton to meet our needs, so be it."

Stuart's face was bright with excitement as he saluted and hastily departed.

Lee resumed pondering what steps he should take to have the best chance of getting his army back to Virginia. As he did so, an alternate plan was taking shape in his mind. Perhaps the entire army should use the bridge at Hancock.

* * *

Vicksburg had surrendered that morning, July 4th, and in Grant's tent, as the sun was dropping below the horizon, he was speaking with Major General William Sherman about the progress of the efforts to transport the large number of Rebel prisoners when the sentry poked his head inside.

Stone bridge typical of those in Maryland and Virginia.
iStock.com

"Excuse me, sir, Admiral Porter is here."

"Have him come in."

As Porter entered, Grant and Sherman rose to greet him. Both were pleased and grateful for the excellent support and cooperation given the army by Rear Admiral Porter and his flotilla of gunboats and monitors.

"General Grant, General Sherman, I have just received directions from Secretary Welles to provide transports for a full corps from your army to be moved to Cincinnati, where they will board trains that will take them to their ultimate destination that will be identified upon their arrival in Baltimore. Mr. Welles also said that General Grant will travel with the corps for a meeting with Mr. Stanton, General Halleck, and the president."

As he spoke, Porter noted the surprised look on each of the generals' faces.

"You haven't received word of this yet?"

A disturbed Grant said, "No, we have not!"

"Well, I expect you will shortly," Porter said. "In the meantime, I will be collecting our transports for you. Should be ready by tomorrow morning." Porter paused as if he had something additional to say, but then smiled, saluted, and left, having apparently decided not to joke with them about the efficiency of Army communications.

Grant said, "Billy, since I am going to be east for an unknown period, I want you to take command of this army and chase down Joe Johnston, and maneuver so as to push on to Atlanta. If Atlanta is taken, the way will be clear to do some heavy damage to the Confederacy's ability to provide needed materiel to the Rebel armies. It will also further damage the interior lines of their system of supply and communications."

The tent flap parted, and an excited young soldier handed Grant a paper containing the message from Halleck which Grant read aloud:

War Department
Washington, July 4, 1863 ---- 3 p.m.
Major-General Grant, Vicksburg:
SIR: At the direction of the President, you will embark one of your corps, including all equipment and train, in such transports as are provided by the navy, for transport by river to Cincinnati, where the corps and all equipment and train will transfer to rail transportation. Also, at the direction of the President, you personally will accompany the corps. Upon arrival Baltimore, the corps will continue to its destination, to be identified at that time, while you will proceed to a meeting with the President, the Secretary of War, and myself. All this to be done once Vicksburg is secured.
H. W. HALLECK
General-in-Chief

As Grant fell silent, obviously pondering the import of what he had just read, Sherman stood up, drawing Grant's attention.

"Do I have a say as to which corps will go east?"

"Well, I suppose you should, seeing as you will be commanding the remaining corps," Grant said as he drew a cigar from an inner pocket of his coat. "Which corps do you have in mind?"

"Ord. Send Ord. I'm guessing this is being done to reinforce Meade, and Meade can be difficult but Ord can handle him."

Grant nodded, "I'll have orders prepared for Ord and the Thirteenth Corps to move out tomorrow when Porter's transports are ready."

Sherman shook hands with Grant, and then quietly spoke with feeling. "Sam, we've been through Hell together. I and this army will miss your leadership, but if you can hasten the war's end by going east, it will be worth it." Saluting, he turned and left.

Grant sat down, lit his cigar, and began thinking about what might await him in Washington. It occurred to him, judging from the last sentence of Halleck's message, that his report of the fall of Vicksburg had not yet reached Washington.

He began writing his acknowledgement of Halleck's message, stating that Vicksburg had surrendered on July 4, and that Ord's corps would commence embarking in Porter's transports with full equipment on the 5th, with arrival Baltimore expected the evening of the 8th. He requested approval for Sherman to move up to command of the army, and closed by saying Porter would be accompanying him, something he had not yet discussed with the admiral. Then his thoughts turned to the situation in the east as he lit a fresh cigar.

Lt. Gen, U.S. Grant, USA
©David John Murphy

* * *

JULY 5, 1863

Williamsport was sleeping as the lead brigade of Pleasonton's cavalry quietly entered the town. Although they had been in the saddle over twelve hours, every trooper was alert, expecting to encounter gray uniforms at any moment, but to their surprise, none appeared. To Brigadier General Wesley Merritt, the lack of any opposition gave him a vague feeling of unease. Surely Lee had taken the precaution of guarding his line of supply with Winchester. Had he been so preoccupied with the events of the past three days that he had overlooked securing his line of supply as well as his means of crossing into Virginia?

Merritt led his brigade down to where the ferry was located and saw how the river had already overflowed its banks and was beginning to pour into the Chesapeake and Ohio Canal that flowed parallel to the Potomac River. He could barely see the ferry barges that were tied to two cables that spanned the river. Cutting the cables took only a few minutes, and Merritt watched as the ends of the cables were carried downstream, releasing the barges to the mercy of the surging floodwater.

Brig. Gen. Wesley Merritt, USA
David John Murphy

That done, Merritt permitted his troopers to rest in some nearby warehouses for what remained of the dark hours, it now being near 3 am, while he set off to report to Pleasonton, whom he found at the top of the hill where the road from Hagerstown led into Williamsport.

Pleasanton was talking to Brigadier General John Buford, who was supervising the First and Second Brigades of his division as they were setting up defensive positions. Seeing Merritt, Pleasonton inquired about the ferry.

"Sir, the ferry cables have been cut, and the barges attached to them were last seen drifting down the river."

"Good. Be sure to destroy the machinery that pulls the cables, after the town has awakened."

"Yes, sir. I gave permission for the men to rest until sunrise. We'll blow up the machinery then." Saluting, Merritt departed, chiding himself for not thinking of the machinery.

As Pleasonton mounted his horse to see how Gregg and the Second Division were faring, he remarked that it was strange that there had been no encounter with any of Stuart's cavalry or any other Rebels. Buford agreed and made a mental note to mount patrols after sunrise, to check the whereabouts of Lee's army.

Maj. Gen., John Buford, USA
©David John Murphy

* * *

Anderson had convinced Hill of the need to rest the troops and had made it clear to the manager of the Monterey House that it was in the manager's best interest to provide food for the men of his division. It was now shortly before dawn, and Wilcox's brigade was forming in column for the ascent to the pass. The rain had stopped, and the troops, rested and fed, were in much better spirits. The hotel had run out of food after serving bacon, ham, bread, potatoes, beans and soup to most of the brigade.

At the order from Anderson, Wilcox and his brigade began the climb up the narrow, rock-strewn road, each step requiring a careful look to avoid the jagged rocks protruding from the roadbed. Wilcox saw how difficult and even dangerous it would have been to have attempted to take the road at night in the pouring rain, and he mentally thanked Anderson for his good judgment in waiting for daylight. As it was, the ascent necessarily proceeded at a very slow tempo, with the wagons carrying what remained of their ammunition requiring constant halts while men and mules strained to get them up the road without breaking a wheel or axle on those blasted rocks.

Almost an hour after starting, the head of the column reached the top, where they met no opposition. As they began the descent, the skies opened with a vengeance, with sheet after sheet of stinging, wind-blown rain, accompanied by bolts of lightning and bursts of thunder.

* * *

Dawn was breaking as Merritt, refreshed by a few hours of sleep and the mug of coffee in his hand, supervised the placement of the explosives around the ferry machinery. Leaving orders to detonate the charges when ready, Merritt mounted and started up the hill on the street that led to Pleasonton's headquarters.

"Mornin', Gen'ril."

Looking up, Merritt saw a man leaning out of a second story window of a building that overlooked the river. Merritt saluted and returned the greeting.

"Looks like them Rebs across the river are trying to find a way to cross," the man said, pointing to the shore opposite Williamsport.

Merritt halted his horse and swung it around to face the river. Uncasing his field glasses, he observed several gray uniforms down by the ferry landing. Behind them, he saw six covered wagons, which he assumed contained ammunition for Lee. As he watched, the distant figures returned to the wagons and turned them around. They showed no sign of having seen him or any of his troopers.

Merritt asked the man in the window to keep watching the Rebs and continued up the hill to report to Pleasonton. Hearing an explosion, he considered it to be the destruction of the ferry machinery noting to himself to include that in his report.

About half a mile ahead of Merritt, Pleasonton was having breakfast when John Buford appeared.

"Sir," said Buford, "recall our conversation yesterday about the absence of Stuart. I have sent out four mounted patrols to reconnoiter the roads north of here to find out where Lee and his army are. The lack of any contact with Stuart bothers me."

"Good. It bothers me too. I ..." Pleasonton was interrupted by the arrival of Merritt.

"Good morning, Generals." Looking at Pleasonton, Merritt continued. "Sir, the ferry machinery has been destroyed, and my brigade is rested, fed, and ready for duty, although the mounts could use more rest and lots more fodder."

"Thank you, Merritt. They should have time to rest and feed the next couple of days." The muted thunder of hoofs caught their attention. To the north, where the road from Hagerstown was located, they saw a group of Union cavalry riding hard toward Williamsport. Buford identified them as one of his patrols.

Turning into town, the group soon appeared, heading toward them. The lieutenant leading the patrol reined in his mount, and without dismounting, saluted and said, "General, there is a brigade-size body of Rebel cavalry over by St. James School, heading at a trot to the crossroads near the school. My guess is that they will take the road to town at the crossroads."

Buford said, "Excuse me, General. I'd best be getting over to my division to get ready for the Rebs' arrival."

As Buford departed, Merritt informed Pleasonton of the sighting of the Rebel wagons opposite Williamsport, including their departure and the man whom he had asked to watch them.

Pleasonton mused for a bit, then he said, "The maps I saw showed several ferries upriver from here as well as a bridge at Hancock. Send a strong patrol up there and destroy those ferries, and send a squadron to Hancock to guard the bridge. If the Rebs get across, we must not let them reach Lee. Maybe your watcher will have some useful information for you."

Merritt cantered into town and saw his lookout intently studying the area across the river. As Merritt approached, the man called out. "Gen'ril, them Rebs are hightailin' it up the road to Hancock, where they'd be crossin' on the stone bridge."

Merritt acknowledged with a salute and spurred his mount to a gallop. When the sentry saw his general racing down the hill, he alerted the sergeant who had the bugler sound "Assembly." Troopers were rapidly falling into formation as Merritt abruptly halted. Still mounted, Merritt called his officers forward. "There are six wagons across the river that are racing upriver, probably bringing ammunition for the Rebs, and probably headed for the bridge at Hancock. We have to intercept them. I will take First and Fifth U.S. to Hancock, Major Haseltine will be in charge here in my absence. All troopers will carry full cartridge boxes. We may run into some of Stuart's people, so be ready. Captain Lord, Captain Mason, we leave in five minutes."

Turning to one of his staff, Merritt continued. "Lieutenant Bixler, assemble a squadron from the Second U. S. and get to Hancock as quickly as possible. Intercept those six wagons from Winchester and destroy them. Any questions?"

With a "No sir!" and a salute, Bixler was gone.

Merritt looked toward Haseltine. "Major, have the Sixth Pennsylvania and the Second U.S. ready to move out in case you are needed to reinforce me. And keep General Pleasonton informed. I will maintain contact with General Buford."

Buford was surveying the disposition of his troopers who were holding the left sector of the defense line set up around Williamsport when he saw Merritt leading a column of cavalry heading west out of Williamsport. Their route brought them close enough for Merritt to leave the column and approach Buford. After informing Buford of his intentions, Merritt asked if any Rebs had been seen on Buford's front.

"The last of the patrols I sent out just returned and saw what they believed to be a strong force, brigade maybe, of cavalry heading west. Likely the same group reported earlier down by St. James School. That was about fifteen minutes ago." Buford paused, looked at the troopers riding by, and added, "You might think about bringing on the rest of your troopers." He paused again. Then, "Come to think of it, with no way to cross at Williamsport now that you wrecked the ferry and the river is still rising, there's no reason for us to be tied up here. The thing now is to keep those wagons from reaching Lee. I will inform Pleasonton of the situation while at the same time moving out to follow you. Have you sent a squadron to Hancock?"

"Yes, sir, they are on the way now, and General, I would appreciate having one of your staff relay my order to Haseltine to join up." Buford nodded, and Merritt galloped off to rejoin his troops.

As the last of Merritt's column passed, the Eighth Illinois of the First Brigade of Buford's division began forming column, and minutes later, they too were on the move, followed by successive regiments as they became ready to go.

Buford was conferring with Colonels Gamble and Devin, his two brigade commanders, when Pleasonton and his staff arrived. Buford quickly dismissed Gamble and Devin, who slipped off to join their troops. Gamble had been told to get to Merritt and advise him of Buford's plan if the Confederates seen by the patrol were heading for Hancock.

To Buford's surprise, Pleasonton agreed with Buford's plan. "You're right, John, Hancock is now the key, not Williamsport. I'll send Gregg's First Brigade to join you while we keep up appearances here. To do that, I will need to keep Haseltine here."

Buford nodded and saluted as Pleasonton rode off to meet with Gregg and Haseltine. Buford looked over at Captain Charles Norris, one of his staff officers.

"Did you hear all that, Charlie?"

"Yes, sir, I did."

"Good. Skedaddle up the road and pass it on to Merritt, Gamble and Devin." Buford's last act before joining his division was to send two couriers to inform Meade of the rapidly changing situation at Williamsport.

* * *

The squadron had arrived at Hancock after a hard ride of about an hour. Lieutenant Bixler was about to eat a sandwich when Sergeant Brooks approached, followed by a young trooper who was holding a note in his gloved hand.

"Sir, this is from General Merritt."

Quickly reading Merritt's note to the effect that the brigade was in route to Hancock, and the absolute need to prevent the wagons from reaching Lee's army, Bixler called the thirty or so troopers to assemble on the double.

Bixler was mentally wishing he had some artillery as he gazed at the bridge. The latter was the typical narrow arched bridge constructed of heavy stone, the type of bridge that was common among the roads of northern Virginia and parts of Maryland. It would not be possible for the squadron to destroy it, so some other way had to be found to either prevent the Confederate wagons from crossing or to destroy the wagons if they managed to get across. As he was musing, Brooks spoke.

"Lieutenant, with that bridge being as narrow as it is, it wouldn't take much to fill it with chopped tree limbs soaked with coal oil. At the right time, we could set them on fire, and then hit the stalled wagons with our carbines and maybe cause the stuff they're carrying to explode."

Bixler agreed immediately, and the troopers went to work on some nearby small trees and within fifteen minutes, the bridge began to fill with branches and dry trash from nearby homes. The showers had ceased for the moment, and as troopers stacked the debris on the bridge, others poured coal oil on each layer.

As the troopers were finishing the work, a lookout reported sighting the wagons moving out of the woods on the muddy lane about a mile from the bridge. The wagons began to slow as they encountered the deep mud of the road that lay unsheltered beneath the sky.

Four troopers-soaked torches with coal oil and crouched behind the barrier of debris with matches ready. The others fanned out on either side of the road to the bridge, taking concealed positions where they could attack the wagons with their carbines. Several of the better marksmen were detailed to hit the drivers, while the others fired at the wagons to attempt to explode their cargoes.

Bixler was watching the wagons with his field glasses when he saw the wagons suddenly stop. Their cavalry escort of about a dozen or so had stopped them and were pointing toward the bridge. Bixler assumed they had spotted the debris.

"Lieutenant! Look!" called a trooper, pointing to a nearby house. A young woman was waving a white towel from an upper window that faced the river. The trooper was about to fire at her, but Bixler shouted, "No! Do not fire!"

"Sir, them cavalry boys are comin' on strong!"

Bixler saw them galloping on the grass on either side of the rain-soaked road. Still watching through his field glasses, Bixler shouted, "Take aim and fire on my command!"

Tense seconds of waiting, then "Fire!" Twenty-five carbines blazed at once, knocking down well over half of the oncoming riders. It was evident that they had not expected such opposition, and the remaining riders, bent low over their saddles, turned and galloped back toward the wagons, managing to avoid any further casualties.

The cries of some of the wounded Confederates could be heard, and Bixler was thinking of calling a truce with whoever was his opposite in gray when a shot rang out, fired by the same trooper who had warned Bixler about the young woman. Quickly looking up, Bixler saw an older man, pistol in hand, slowly topple forward through that same open window.

The man lay inertly on the soft ground, pistol still gripped in his right hand. Bixler could see that he was breathing. He started to approach him when he saw the man begin to raise his hand holding the gun.

"Father! No!" screamed the young woman now outside the house as she ran to her father. He dropped the pistol and began sobbing as his daughter knelt beside him. The girl looked up at Bixler. "My brother was one of those who was shot by your men." Then she burst into tears.

Bixler's mind was racing, but now he fixed mentally on the over-riding objective of destroying the wagons and their contents. The note from Merritt warned of possible Rebel cavalry in the area, and Bixler knew he had to act quickly.

"Sergeant, have the men clear a path through that stuff on the bridge. We need to get over there and get those wagons. General Merritt said there may be Reb cavalry coming here, so I want you and the torchers to stay here, but on the other side to keep them from coming after us, at least until we can destroy those wagons. "

The men dug in and soon, there was a path wide enough for a horse and rider to pass through. Led by Bixler, they crossed in quick order, with the sergeant and his four torchers closing the path as the last troopers crossed over.

Bixler pointed his right arm forward, and the race began. The wagon drivers were having difficulty turning the wagons around in the deep, sticky mud. The six cavalrymen, who were all that remained of the escort force of 22 men, looked at the wagons, then looked at the rapidly approaching Yankees. The corporal said, "Let's git!" and they quickly disappeared into the woods.

Bixler arrived at the wagons shortly afterwards and was greeted by the driver of the lead wagon.

"Well, Lieutenant, guess y'all done bagged us."

"Kinda looks that way. What's in the wagons?"

"Guess ya could say they's 'nuff bullets and powder to blow up an army!"

As the laughter subsided, Bixler said, "Well, I guess we'll just blow up some wagons. You boys should clear outta here."

With the help of the troopers, some of the mounts left riderless by the skirmish at the bridge were rounded up, and the drivers, tipping their hats, took off.

Bixler and the troopers made a quick check of the wagons, noting that the contents were all marked U. S., some of the bullets and powder lost when Ewell whipped Milroy at Winchester in June while on the way to invade Pennsylvania with the rest of Lee's army.

Using fuses from those found in one of the wagons, they set two five-minute fuses in each wagon, lit them, and rode back to the bridge. They dismounted and waited, holding their horses to steady them when the wagons blew. They saw the wagons erupt in huge balls of flame, quickly followed by a rush of hot air and the loudest explosion that any had ever heard. Debris, some burning, was falling on the field and the woods, with a few pieces landing near the group. The horses took it well, and they crossed back into Maryland, Sergeant Brooks and his torchers having again cleared a path.

Depending on atmospheric conditions, sound may be heard at a far location while not being heard at all at a near location. Such was the case with the wagons' explosion. Brigadier General Fitzhugh Lee, commanding a brigade of Stuart's cavalry division, Army of Northern Virginia, was leading his brigade to occupy Hancock, and was less than five miles away when the explosion occurred, yet neither he nor any of his command heard it.

And with the heavy dark clouds overhead, they failed to notice the pall of smoke rising from the burning wagons.

On the other hand, Merritt, who was some eighteen miles from Hancock, heard the sharp bang very clearly, and rightly surmised that Lieutenant Bixler and his squadron had intercepted and destroyed the ammunition resupply from Winchester. He accordingly slowed the troopers to a walk, and sent a courier back to inform Buford, Pleasonton, and Meade. He had just sent the courier off when one of his advanced scouts came riding hard over the slight rise ahead and obviously had some urgent information for Merritt.

"Sir, about fifteen miles ahead I saw what looked to be an entire brigade of Rebel cavalry, heading for Hancock. That was about a half hour ago, so I reckon they're close to Hancock by now. They were moving at a good pace."

Merritt halted his force. His first thought was that the Confederates, having heard the explosion, would have gone to a gallop and likely were at Hancock now. His next thought was of Bixler and his troopers; what was happening with them? In any case, he decided to await the arrival of Buford as well as the rest of his brigade.

* * *

Sergeant Brooks was asking Bixler about removing the oil-soaked limbs from the bridge when he heard a trooper exclaim, "Good God, it's the Rebel army!" Looking over where the trooper was pointing, Bixler and Brooks simultaneously shouted for troopers to mount and ride back into Virginia. The rain had just begun to fall again as the troopers lashed their mounts through the path still open on the bridge.

Shouts from the Rebels were punctuated by the reports of small arms as the lead elements of Lee's brigade charged toward the bridge. Brooks was the last to cross, and lighting a torch as he crossed, he tossed it onto the pile which blossomed quickly into a roaring mass of flames, singeing the back of his neck.

Bending low in the saddle, Brooks heard more gunshots. The rider off to his right slumped forward and began to slide off his saddle. Brooks tried to grab his arm but couldn't quite reach Jackson, the trooper who had been hit. Jackson fell to the ground, tumbling several times, and then was still. Brooks pulled up, and looking back, saw the Rebels dousing the flames, aided now by the heavy rain. Jackson was not moving, and concluding the trooper was dead, Brooks spurred his mount to catch up with the squadron that was now in the woods. Jackson was one of the best in the squadron, and Brooks cursed the bullet that had killed him.

* * *

Generals Howard and Hays were conferring with their engineers regarding the best use of the terrain in deciding the location of the fortified line that would stretch across the neck of the peninsula opposite Williamsport, when they were interrupted by the heavy bang of the exploding wagons, coming from the northwest. Howard's cavalry escort consisted of two companies of the First Indiana Cavalry, commanded by Captain Abram Sharra.

Sharra happened to be nearby, so Howard gestured for Sharra to join him.

"Captain, take some of your troopers and see what caused that blast we just heard. As you see here on this map, this road that heads into the trees over there goes to Hancock. The map shows a stone bridge at Hancock, and if the bridge has been damaged, we need to know that. "

The two Union corps had arrived shortly after noon, and men and equipment had been off-loaded within two hours. Officers and sergeants were busily getting tents erected and field kitchens set up. With the shoes, clothing and ammunition supplied them when they had arrived at Westminster the day before, their morale had improved in like measure. The sleep they enjoyed during the train trip also added to their feeling like new men. But the fortunes of war were about to end their period of respite.

* * *

When Meade received Pleasonton's report concerning Hancock, he was faced with the decision to relegate Williamsport to secondary importance and move to hold Lee at Hancock or continue with the original plan. By Lee establishing his base at Hagerstown, he could go either way once the river fell back to its normal depth. If Meade moved to block Hancock, Lee could slip across at Williamsport, and vice versa, or he could head for Baltimore or Washington. Then came the message from Merritt that Fitz Lee's brigade had taken Hancock. Was this a ruse to draw Meade away from Williamsport?

Meade continued studying the map when suddenly he saw the move he should make in the developing game of chess with Lee. If Pleasonton occupied Williamsport, and with Sykes and Sedgwick blocking a crossing at Shepherdstown, Lee must either turn and attack Meade or go west to Hancock. With Williamsport seized, there was no need for the block by Howard and Hays across the river from Williamsport.

Meade sent the following message to Howard by way of the station at Harpers Ferry:

HEADQUARTERS, ARMY OF THE POTOMAC, JULY 5, 1863

Maj. Gen. Howard:

Williamsport now being occupied by Pleasonton, assume Lee will attempt to cross at Hancock. You are therefore directed to proceed to Hancock, now held by Fitz Lee's brigade of cavalry. Seize Hancock and hold until arrival of Ninth Corps expected on July 7. I will send additional artillery by fastest means available, as well as more rounds, for purpose of destroying stone bridge at Hancock, if possible.

GEORGE MEADE, Major General Commanding

* * *

Lee was riding Traveler in company with Longstreet when the trooper from Fitz Lee's brigade arrived with the news that Hancock was now occupied but the ammunition resupply had been destroyed by a contingent of Union cavalry. However, the bridge at Hancock was intact. Lee sent the trooper back with a note instructing Fitz Lee to urgently request more ammunition from Winchester, and to dig in at Hancock until Anderson's division, now arriving at the outskirts of Hagerstown, relieved him.

Longstreet asked Lee if he now intended to cross at Hancock instead of Williamsport.

"It depends on what Meade does. I want us to be ready to move either way once the river recedes. As soon as I can set up headquarters in

Hagerstown, I want to meet with you and Hill to work out how best to dispose your corps for such a move."

Longstreet was not sure that he had heard Lee correctly. "Sir, did you omit Ewell, or did I miss some of what you said?"

"No, you heard me correctly. Ewell will be busy with rear guard matters while we meet."

Seemingly out of nowhere, a man in civilian attire appeared and rode up to Longstreet, who obviously knew him. The two of them rode off to one side, and Longstreet listened intently as the man spoke. He handed Longstreet some newspapers, saluted, and departed. Longstreet rejoined Lee, who was waiting to hear the information that Longstreet had received.

"The Ninth Corps has been ordered to come east by train from Kentucky to bolster Meade and is expected to arrive in two days. There are also rumors that some of Grant's army will be coming east, now that Vicksburg has fallen."

"Vicksburg has surrendered? When did this happen?"

"Yesterday, according to the newspapers. Johnston was unable to draw off Grant, so Pemberton surrendered."

Both rode silently for several minutes, then Lee spoke. "We must act all the sooner, before Meade receives these reinforcements. We cannot wait for the river to recede. That means we will have to cross at Hancock, but we must make Meade think that our real objective is Williamsport."

Lee called out to his aide, Walter Taylor, who was riding nearby as usual. "Now that the rain has stopped, we must move along more quickly. Inform General Hill to get his corps into Hagerstown as rapidly as possible and set up defenses on the eastern and southern edges of town."

Turning to Longstreet, "Ammunition?"

"One day of combat, maybe a half day more." Longstreet turned away and began issuing orders to pick up the pace. As he did so, the question lingered in his mind: what did Lee have in store for Dick Ewell?

* * *

General Imboden and his very long train of wagons had just arrived at Greencastle when the courier arrived with the note directing him to avoid

Williamsport and proceed to Hancock without delay, using the Hancock bridge to cross into Virginia. He was several miles behind the head of the train, which was started on the road to Williamsport.

Imboden having ordered the wagons that were just arriving at the turn in Greencastle to head for Hancock, he had the back-tracking wagons fall in at the end of the train.

As they waited, some of the town folk engaged the drivers in conversation and offered them some sandwiches and coffee for themselves and for the wounded. It was during the conversation that one of the locals mentioned Vicksburg had surrendered, news that shocked the wounded officers and enlisted in the wagons nearby. A cloud of gloom descended as the chatting ceased.

Imboden also soon learned of Vicksburg's fall and assumed the change in routing must somehow be a result. He had been expecting Pemberton to surrender, but the news was still disheartening. Refocusing on his responsibilities with the thousands of wounded, the four thousand Union prisoners guarded by the remnant of Pickett's division, and the herds of cattle and sheep that were now passing through Greencastle, he sent the word to all wagons and to the unit leaders of his 2100 cavalry troopers that they must continue moving until they crossed into Virginia at Hancock.

Imboden was beginning to feel some excitement at the prospect of finally gaining relief from the constant threat of Union cavalry attacks; little did he realize the ordeal that awaited him.

* * *

Captain Sharra and his twenty troopers were passing through the heavily wooded area that extended some twenty miles from just west of Hedgesville to a point about a mile south of Hancock. They had been riding for almost an hour, and as they proceeded along the road, Sharra considered it ideal for an ambush. He ordered the troop to move in single file, at extended interval, with carbines ready. The road was straight, providing a clear view down the long tunnel of over-arching tree branches. The leading trooper suddenly halted as he raised his arm, pointing down the road. There, in the distance, were riders moving at a canter, riders in the blue uniform of Union cavalry.

Moving out in front, Sharra ordered his troopers to move out, and the two groups quickly closed the distance between them. Sharra and Bixler were acquainted, and after exchanging greetings, Bixler gave an account of the destruction of the wagons, and their narrow escape from Fitz Lee's boys.

"Is the bridge intact?"

"Not only is it intact, it's also firmly held by the Rebels."

An hour later, Sharra and Bixler were informing Generals Howard and Hays of the situation at Hancock when a sergeant holding a message interrupted.

"Sir, orders from General Meade."

After reading the message and handing it to Hays, Howard addressed Bixler. "Lieutenant, did you have time to gain some familiarity with the area around Hancock?"

"Yes, sir, a bit." Bixler described the setting of the bridge, the houses in the vicinity, the mile or so clear approach to the bridge on the Virginia side, and the heavy stone construction of the bridge.

Hays spoke. "The woods can hide the approach of our troops, especially if we move out, say, two hours before sunset so as to be in place to storm the bridge just at daybreak."

"General, that bridge is fairly narrow, not as wide as the Antietam bridge, and with flooded banks around it, there's no way to get across except over the bridge. That's true for anyone trying to cross from either side. We don't need to seize the bridge. A battery of a couple long range artillery pieces and some sharpshooters should be able to prevent any crossing attempt as long as the river is high."

"Thank you, Lieutenant, that's good to know," said Howard. "General, looks like we have some work to do."

* * *

JULY 6, 1863

Fitz Lee was not happy. He had volunteered for the cavalry because he disliked the boredom of camp life and the idea of fighting on foot. The dash and slash of a cavalry charge was much the better way to fight a battle, with him and his mount as one, cutting down the foe. Yet here he was, assigned the onerous (to him) task of holding this bridge in this God-forsaken village.

It was still an hour or so before dawn, and not being able to sleep due to his frustrated mood, Lee was wandering somewhat aimlessly, checking the defensive works thrown up by his troopers, works that showed their lack of experience in static warfare. He made a mental note to conduct a thorough inspection after breakfast, his sense of duty over-riding his dislike for the situation.

The sergeant of the guard approached him, extending a mug of hot black coffee that Lee accepted with thanks.

"This ain't much of a bridge for an army to cross over, sir. Too danged narrow, as I see it."

Brig. Gen. Fitzhugh
"Fitz" Lee, CSA
©David John Murphy

Lee had been too disgruntled to have taken notice, but now, as he sipped his coffee, he walked over to the bridge and, for the first time, saw that the bridge was indeed narrow, about a third less width than bridges elsewhere. He wondered if General Lee was aware of its width.

"You're right, Sergeant, it is pretty danged narrow. Is Major Hotchkiss still here?"

"Yes, sir, he's sleeping over yonder, and asked to be woke up at 4 a.m."

Lee checked his watch, noting it was almost 3:30. "Wake him now and ask him to join me at the bridge."

In a few minutes, a still drowsy Hotchkiss approached Lee, who was standing by the shallow flow of the flooded river over the end of the bridge.

"Mornin', Jed. Sorry to interrupt your sleep. Sergeant Watts brought my attention to the narrow width of this bridge. Would you measure it and make a sketch that shows its dimensions, to be given to General Lee when you return this morning."

"Sir, I have already done that and if you think it's urgent, I'll be on my way in half an hour."

Smiling, Lee said, "Jed, you're always way ahead of the rest of us. And so is General Lee. I should have guessed that he sent you here just for that reason, " nodding toward the bridge.

Answering the smile with a grin, Hotchkiss saluted and was gone.

Fitz Lee was beginning to be in a better mood, anticipating being ordered to leave Hancock, once General Lee saw the size of the bridge.

* * *

On the south side of the Potomac, the Second Division of the Eleventh Corps and the Third Division of the Second Corps had been marching throughout the night, accompanied by artillery consisting of twelve guns from the Eleventh Corps and twelve from the Second Corps. They had started just after sunset and were now beginning to file out of the dense woods that covered most of the road to Hancock, opening into a field a mile or so south of the bridge.

Dawn was an hour away, and the troops quietly began to erect earthworks of mud and logs, the noise of their work being lost in the heavy downpour that had begun the previous afternoon. Under the watchful eye of Brigadier General William Hays, the Second Corps commander, a zigzag line of breastworks and trench steadily took shape, extending across both the road up the Cumberland Valley and the road to Martinsburg.

As daylight filtered through the clouds and the rain, Fitz Lee's troopers awoke to the astonishing sight of the Yankee line of fortifications. To make matters worse, the 24 Union guns began systematically pounding the stone bridge with solid shot fired in a high arc like a giant curveball.

Fitz Lee's good mood quickly disappeared.

* * *

After receiving Hotchkiss's report, Robert E. Lee had not considered the width of the Hancock bridge to necessarily be a problem, unless faced with strong opposition on the Virginia side, expecting none until the Union Ninth Corps arrived, which was not due for another day, according to the estimate made by his railroad people. If all went according to his plan, Lee would have crossed the day before the arrival of the Ninth Corps.

Now, sitting in the United States Hotel in Hagerstown, he was surprised at the initiative shown by Meade in putting some of his army across the Potomac. The report from Fitz Lee had added the information about the artillery pounding the bridge, a development he had not considered in his planning. He had under-estimated Meade, and Meade had now stolen the initiative.

Studying the map, he mentally placed Meade's forces as reported by Stuart, and saw two corps in the Sharpsburg area, Pleasonton in Williamsport, one or two corps across the river, and Meade's logistics base at Frederick, Maryland, the latter guarded by French's division of about 5,000 men. That left three or four corps pursuing Lee's army. By his rough estimate, Lee's 35,000 effectives were being pursued by an equal number or perhaps even less. He had not considered Meade to be a gambler willing to take much risk, but now he realized that Meade had taken a large gamble, splitting his army and no doubt counting on Parke to reduce the risk once he arrived. Lee's opinion of Meade rose even higher, but at the same time, Lee began estimating how he could take advantage of Meade's gamble.

While Lee was pondering his next move, Longstreet's corps was moving through the streets of Hagerstown, their ragged appearance matching that of Hill's corps which had passed through earlier. Despite the rain, many of the locals had come out to see these Rebels, these Southrons who had so jauntily marched into Maryland and Pennsylvania just ten days earlier. Seeing some young boys eating apples, one bronzed Rebel stopped and asked them where he could get an apple.

"Here, mister, you can have this one," one of the boys replied, reaching into a bag he was holding. The soldier thanked him and gave him a minie ball from his cartridge box. The boys were delighted, and excitedly took off to show their prize at home. A bystander, witnessing the exchange, traded smiles with the soldier and could not help wishing the man well.

"Where are you from, sir?" he asked the soldier.

"Grew up on a farm near Annapolis, and didn't agree with Mr. Lincoln ordering an invasion of the southern states, so here I am. My older brother is in the Union army. Sure hope he's not among the casualties." With a wave of his hand, he rejoined his unit. The elderly bystander sighed, imagining the anxiety that surely plagued the soldier's parents.

* * *

Like his adversary Lee, Meade was weighing the situation, and he also realized the gamble he was taking with the disposition of his forces. Much depended on the river and the weather. If the rain continued for another day or so, Lee would either have to dig in or try to fight his way out. Meade would welcome the former, and he felt he could hold out long enough for reinforcements to arrive if the latter occurred. If the rain stopped anytime soon, he figured Lee would likely wait for the river to go down and then would try to cross. Locals said it took about a day for the depth to reach a level shallow enough for fording.

After further study of his forces and their various locations, Meade decided to move Fifth Corps from Sharpsburg north to Tappans where the National Pike running southeast from Hagerstown intersected the road heading east-southeast from Williamsport; Sixth Corps would move north to Wagner's Crossroad; and Pleasonton was to move south out of Williamsport and take position at Downs. With Twelfth Corps directly behind Ewell, just west of Cavetown, and First and Third Corps at Leitersburg, Meade was tightening the arc around Lee, and his forces would be better placed to aid one another. Kilpatrick, after weathering one of Meade's famous temper outbursts, was diligently moving patrols of cavalry to keep Meade informed of the Rebel army's movement, although he still itched to hit that long train of wagons led by Imboden.

Buford, with his First and Second Brigades, had just arrived at Williamsport when Pleasonton informed him to be ready to move south to Downs at 6 pm as ordered by General Meade, where they would then connect with Fifth Corps at Tappans.

Judging that Merritt was still some fifteen miles from Williamsport, Buford sent a rider with instructions for Merritt to expedite his return, stating the reason why, but Merritt was never to get the order.

* * *

Merritt was approaching the area of Indian Springs, moving at normal pace, when a youngster came over the rise ahead, riding a big draft horse. Upon seeing the blue uniforms, the youngster spurred toward Merritt, waving his arm and shouting.

Hauling up alongside Merritt, the lad excitedly informed Merritt that a large wagon train of Rebels was heading west on the road out of Indian Springs and was just a few miles away.

"Did you see any Rebel cavalry with the wagons?" Merritt asked.

"Yes, sir, sure did. They were riding on either side of the wagons, maybe about a whole hundred of them."

Merritt recalled a fork in the road about two miles ahead, where the road to Indian Springs turned off to the higher ground to his left. The road immediately ahead rose some fifty feet in a sharp rise that concealed the view of anyone coming from the east of it. Merritt spread two regiments, dismounted, on either side of the road along the ridge line, and placed his remaining regiments, mounted, in a clearance several hundred yards to the rear. Using the concealment afforded by a small copse of trees atop the ridge, Merritt took station, awaiting the oncoming wagon train. The dismounted troopers were told to hold fire until Merritt fired his pistol.

After fifteen minutes or so of tense waiting, Merritt saw the head of the wagon train coming down the road, perhaps a mile distant. They were led by troopers who were riding in a loose column, thirty or so, by Merritt's estimate, information he relayed to his troops.

On they came, the noise of the horses and wagons slowly growing. Carbines were cocked, and the tension was palpable. More minutes passed, and when the column of troopers was less than fifty yards away, Merritt cocked his pistol, took aim at the officer leading the Confederates, and fired.

The startled Rebels halted, and within seconds, several hundred carbines opened fire from both sides of the road. The group of troopers in gray were badly hit, the few still in their saddles quickly turned and galloped to the rear, shouting warnings of the ambush. The driver of the leading wagon had been killed in the first volley, and that wagon was blocking the road, with little room to bring the following wagons around it.

Merritt now had the bugler sound the call for the mounted regiments to charge down the road, cutting out wagons as they went, but being alert for encounters with Imboden's troopers. With a train that was seventeen miles in length to guard, the Confederate cavalry were spread for that distance and were being picked off by the advancing Yankee force.

* * *

General Imboden was riding into Indian Springs, chatting with his brother, Colonel George Imboden, commanding the Eighteenth Virginia Cavalry, when the sound of gunfire interrupted him. Imboden knew immediately that his fear of being attacked had been realized. If that were so at this location, the bridge at Hancock must be in enemy hands. The road at Indian Springs widened sufficiently for the wagons to turn, but there was no room for those farther back without considerable effort in backing and turning.

"George, Colonel Smith and his infantry are just a mile back. Have them double time up here and form for battle, so we can save the wagons between here and the tail. Then get word to the rear wagons to turn back and head for Hagerstown, and I'll do the same here. But first we have to stop whoever is attacking us up ahead."

* * *

Merritt was remounting his dismounted regiments when a trooper arrived with the information that they had run into Rebel infantry in Indian Springs and were stalled in cutting out any more wagons until they could overcome the infantry.

Destruction of Merritt's brigade by Fitz Lee and Stuart.
iStock.com

After ordering the remounted regiments to guard those captured wagons holding wounded and burning those containing material of any kind, including food or ammunition, Merritt galloped up the road and soon arrived where his troopers were engaged in exchanging fire with the enemy who were blocking the road just east of Indian Springs. He saw the wagons had turned around and were moving away rapidly. He also noted that the opposing force was being reinforced by a steady trickle of Confederate cavalry. His cavalry had taken heavy initial casualties when they had run into the enemy infantry, and several hundred were now in need of medical help. With Fitz Lee's brigade only ten miles behind him, and the need to get his wounded and killed, as well as the captured Confederate wounded and their wagons within friendly lines, he decided to fall back to the fork in the road and proceed on to Williamsport.

Seeing the Federals retreating, the Confederates let out a triumphal whoop, but were content to let them go. Colonel Smith had at one point mentally prepared to surrender, once the wagon train was gone, and he now was relieved at seeing the Yankees depart. His men had a stiff march awaiting in order to rejoin the train, but better that than being prisoners of the Yankees.

Imboden had managed to get the wagons turned and moving toward Hagerstown, some twenty miles to the east.

* * *

General Buford glanced again at his watch. The time was nearing 5:30 pm and there was still no sign of Merritt. Nor had the trooper he had sent yet returned. If Merritt had received his message he should have arrived by now, unless he had run into trouble of some kind. Or the trooper he had sent had fallen into Rebel hands. He had informed Pleasonton of the situation earlier, and Pleasonton said they would move out on schedule, leaving word in Williamsport for Merritt to join them at Downs. Buford understood the need to carry out Meade's order, but that did not allay his concern. Where the devil was Merritt?

* * *

The bridge at Hancock finally yielded to the Yankee artillery, and once the center stones began to give way, the entire span crumbled into the torrent below, to the cheers of the Yankee gunners.

Fitz Lee watched with mixed reaction. On the one hand, Lee had lost an alternate means of escape, but on the other hand (for Fitz Lee at least) the onerous chore of being tied to Hancock no longer existed, and he and his brigade could return to the real business of the cavalry.

The bugler sounded "Boots and Saddles," and twenty minutes later, Fitz Lee led his troopers out of Hancock. He was not concerned about the loss of the bridge; he had no doubts about Robert E. Lee 's ability to get them back to Virginia.

* * *

At the same time, Merritt was taking his brigade south out of Indian Springs, moving slower than their normal pace due to the wagons that numbered exactly 113. The moaning and groaning of the wounded Confederates as the wagons bounced along was also bothering him. He was tempted to release those wagons containing only wounded, and the more he thought about it, he realized that keeping only the seven wagons filled with a mix of records and weapons, as well as some fifty cases of ammunition, was the expedient thing to do. (He had countered his original order to destroy them.) The wagons were just beginning to turn onto the road from Indian Springs when they were told they were free to rejoin General Imboden, except for the seven not carrying any wounded. These wagons were manned by troopers, and Merritt gave the order to move out. The time was about 5:30 pm.

* * *

Once the train of wagons was moving toward Hagerstown, General Imboden rode ahead to alert General Lee of the imminent arrival of the wagon train with its huge mass of bleating sheep, restless cattle and 4,000 Union prisoners guarded by the survivors of Pickett's division.

As Lee was weighing the consequences of Imboden's decision, a telegrapher brought Lee a message from Fitz Lee informing R. E. Lee of the destruction of the Hancock bridge, and that Fitz's brigade was returning to General Stuart for cavalry duty.

When Lee read the message, he unfolded his map and said, "I think Merritt is trapped. Walter, is Stuart in town or is he out scouting the enemy?"

"He's in town, General. Shall I fetch him?"

"Give him the details of Merritt's situation and tell him this appears to be an opportunity to eliminate a brigade of enemy cavalry. He should work out a quick tactical plan to hit Merritt on the front side while Fitz hits them in the rear. "

Stuart was on the move at 5:45 pm. Stuart had sent a trooper to Fitz Lee to inform him of the pending action, and Fitz had acknowledged stating that they were on the way to attack Merritt's rear, with an estimated time of twenty minutes to arrive on the rear of the Union brigade.

Riding ahead of Hampton's Brigade, Stuart raised his arm, signaling that he had sighted the Union brigade. He expected to see them riding alongside the wagons, instead they were in column and were moving at a good pace, unencumbered by any large group of wagons. Estimating the situation as one requiring immediate action to prevent Merritt from escaping the annihilation Stuart had planned, he had the bugler sound the charge. He would be hitting the Union troopers head-on at a full gallop.

* * *

Merritt saw Stuart just as the Confederate charge began. His seasoned veterans immediately swung into line of battle, a maneuver they executed smoothly and with precision.

With a heavy clash of horses and saber-wielding riders, the ensuing melee quickly became a tangled mass of men and steeds, flashing pistols and swinging sabers delivering death and mayhem. Oncoming ranks of riders on both sides quickly widened the field of battle.

Merritt's troopers were holding up well, but then they were smashed hard in the rear by Fitz Lee's brigade. Outnumbered and surrounded, the blue ranks suddenly gave way, and pocket after pocket began surrendering.

In the confusion and chaos of the battle, several hundred managed to escape, but the brigade as such no longer existed. Among those who escaped was Brigadier General Wesley Merritt, who was mentally berating himself for forgetting that Fitz Lee was behind him and for attacking Imboden's wagon train. If not for the latter, he and his brigade would have arrived at Williamsport well ahead of Fitz Lee.

The rain had slackened earlier in the day, but it now began to fall heavily, with the sky darkened by heavy clouds across which bolts of lightning streaked, accompanied by bangs of thunder, as if the gods were having their own battle in the heavens. It was the storm that aided Merritt and the others to escape, and it shielded them from the eyes of lookouts posted by Longstreet in the several church steeples of Hagerstown. It also covered the departure of Pleasonton and Buford from Williamsport.

A disheartened Merritt arrived in Williamsport about half an hour after the departure of Buford, who had delayed as long as he could, hoping to be there when Merritt's brigade returned. When Merritt failed to appear by 7 pm, Buford could delay no longer. He left three troopers behind with instructions for Merritt to proceed to Downs.

The darkened sky made it seem as if the sun were setting early, and in the gloom, Merritt and the three troopers almost missed meeting. The sergeant in charge of the three-man contingent kept looking down the road on which Merritt and his remnant of the brigade had arrived, obviously expecting to see the rest of the brigade.

Merritt said, "Sergeant, this is all that remains of my brigade. We had better get moving."

A puzzled sergeant replied, "Yes, sir." As they made their way out of town, Merritt began recounting the day's events for the sergeant, using the conversation to rehearse what he would say to Buford and Pleasonton. He knew that he would face a court of inquiry, that likely would recommend a court-martial to determine if Merritt warranted disciplinary action. In the meantime, Merritt reminded himself, there was a war still being fought, and his West Point training disciplined his thinking to concentrate on that.

* * *

Meade had received the daily reports from all corps commanders and was now awaiting the report from his cavalry chief. It was after 8 pm and darkness was setting in. He was getting ready to send a reminder to Pleasonton when Captain Roberts, the staff duty officer, entered his tent with a message in hand. Noting the sober look on Roberts' face, Meade took the message and began to read. The news was both good and bad, mostly bad he concluded after reading of Merritt's loss. He could not help wishing that it had been that impetuous Custer or the equally impetuous Kilpatrick instead of Merritt, but such was the irony of war.

The loss of Merritt's brigade was not a serious loss, but it was a loss nonetheless. However, legal proceedings could wait until the matter at hand was settled. He would have a talk with Merritt and get him onto some sort of special tasking; the Army needed to keep good officers like Merritt who, Meade was certain, had learned a painful lesson that he would never forget, and would be a better officer for having done so.

* * *

Lee listened to Stuart's exuberant report of the battle at Big Spring, with a happy Fitz Lee adding his part. While pleased with the outcome, Lee knew that the biggest benefit was the boost in morale it occasioned, for it did little toward getting his army into Virginia and added to the burden caused by the prisoners. Expressing his congratulations, Lee dismissed Stuart and Fitz Lee, turning his thoughts to the problem of getting his army across the Potomac. Lee was still pondering his problem when the town clock struck midnight.

JULY 7, 1863

The exceptional skill of General Haupt in organizing transportation was exemplified in his speedy movement of the Ninth Corps.

It was still dark when the trains carrying the Ninth began arriving at Martinsburg, where they were met by General Howard. As Howard watched the trains unload, he saw General Parke step down from the passenger car that carried Parke and his staff. Howard dismounted and walked over to the car.

"Good morning, General Parke, and welcome to the Army of the Potomac."

Recognizing Howard by his missing arm, Parke saluted and they shook hands. "Good morning, General. Thank you for meeting us at this early hour."

Howard led Parke and his staff to his tent, where hot coffee awaited them.

A table on one side of the tent held a map showing the disposition of the Union forces commanded by Howard. Parke quickly noted the two divisions at Hancock and asked if it was expected that Lee might cross at that location. Howard described the events that had led to the destruction of the bridge and added that Hays and the two divisions were returning to the lines opposite Williamsport and should be arriving shortly after daybreak.

Pointing to Falling Waters, Howard went on. "This is where Lee had left a pontoon bridge as another means of returning to Virginia. It was cut loose by some of French's cavalry, and with the destruction of the several other ferries between Williamsport and Hancock, as well as the ferry at Williamsport, Lee will have to wait for the river to recede in order to use the fords available, and from the way the rains are continuing, he may have to wait longer than he would like. It is General Meade's intention to seal the Rebel army and hold them until they are forced to surrender or try to fight their way out. Your corps and the corps coming from Grant's army will considerably strengthen our lines, and we should be able to withstand any attack by Lee. We know that Lee has only enough ammunition for one day of combat, so if he does attack, it will be an all or nothing effort. I expect him to attack, but where and when is the question. With the bridge destroyed at Hancock, my guess is that he will try to break out through the southern sector of our lines, but he is a crafty foe and may attack somewhere else. "

* * *

It had been another restless night for Lee. The loss of the bridge at Hancock and the destruction of the ferries in the area had severely reduced his options, and the continuing rain meant the flooded river would not recede soon. The news of a corps coming from Kentucky, together with the still unverified rumor of another corps being brought from Vicksburg, indicated the need to break out now, but even if they did so, he still needed to cross the Potomac, and that raised the need for a pontoon bridge. He had sent two of his young staff officers to reconnoiter the forces across from Williamsport.

Swimming across at night, they had identified the Second and Eleventh Corps. Lee estimated that they were no stronger than 10,000 to 12,000 men, enough to make crossing difficult, but if he could surprise them with a night crossing, he just might be able to get enough troops over to hold the bridgehead. A plan began to take shape in his mind, and he relaxed for a few hours of much needed sleep.

* * *

Meade awoke to the sound of bugles announcing another day. As he donned his uniform, Warren, his acting chief of staff, arrived.

"Good morning, sir. You will be pleased to know that Ninth Corps arrived early this morning. I have a message from Howard requesting any instructions you may have as to the placement of the Ninth. If not otherwise directed, he plans to put them at the Falling Waters crossing where Lee had his pontoon bridge."

Meade walked over to the map pinned to a pole. "Do you know if the bridge at Hancock can be rebuilt quickly, or is it too badly damaged to allow that?"

"Sir, I will have to get that information from Howard."

"Alright. In the meantime, Howard can go ahead with placing Ninth Corps at Falling Waters. I would like to have the Hancock information as soon as possible."

After Warren departed, Meade continued studying the map. He assumed that Stuart's probes had identified the disposition of the Union corps on this side of the river, and Lee had deduced that Second and Eleventh Corps must be across the river. With that knowledge what would Lee do? And did Lee know that another corps was coming? Certainly, his scouts would identify Ninth Corps once they were seen. What would Lee's reaction be? Given Lee's situation, what were his options? Meade decided that he needed to confer with his corps commanders.

* * *

Grant sat in the wardroom of the *River Queen*, the steamboat that Rear Admiral Porter had commandeered for the trip to Cincinnati. He was sipping a cup of coffee and was about to light his third cigar of the morning when Porter entered.

"Good morning, General. Have you had breakfast?"

"Yes, thank you, Admiral," Grant replied, removing the cigar from his mouth. Gazing at the cigar, Grant continued. "When we arrive at Cincinnati, Haupt has arranged a special train for me to get me to Baltimore well ahead of Ord and his corps. That's to give me more time with the President, who undoubtedly is going to have a bushel of questions about Vicksburg. I think you should be there also to speak for the Navy, since you and your boats, sorry, ships played such an important role." Grant looked up at Porter, raising his eyebrows questioningly.

Troop transport on the Mississippi.
iStock.com

Porter had been wondering why Grant had insisted upon his accompanying him on the trip up the river and had guessed it was a precaution on Grant's part in case a situation arose that Grant felt an Army man might not be able to handle. Porter was surprised by Grant's offer, and pleasantly so. Smiling, he replied, "General, your offer is most kind, and I accept, with the request that I have your permission to inform Secretary Welles."

"Of course, by all means." With that, Grant struck a match and lit his cigar, filling the wardroom with pungent cigar smoke. He and Porter then started discussing possible questions that might be asked. But Grant felt a sub-conscious nagging that was generated by his need to be informed about the situation along the Potomac. After a half hour or so, he and Porter considered that they had covered all the areas that might be brought up and Grant arose, stretching his arms while still gripping the butt of his cigar in his teeth.

Going out on deck, Grant tossed his cigar butt overboard and, leaning on the rail, he mentally reviewed what he knew of the situation back east. From reading news reports in the papers picked up at Cairo, Illinois yesterday, he knew that Lee was pinned between the flooded Potomac and Meade, but he needed to know the condition of the two armies after their grueling combat at Gettysburg, the morale of the troops, the state of their logistics, ammunition, weapons. He also needed to know much more about Meade.

And then there was Lee, known to Grant only by his reputation. Was he as formidable as his admirers claimed, or had he just been lucky by having opponents whose ineptitude would make anyone seem invincible? Grant resolved to make time for a thorough briefing while he was in Baltimore, even if it would mean being briefed by Halleck.

* * *

Merritt, weary and dejected, stood before Buford, recounting his encounter with Imboden, followed by the engagement of Stuart on his front and Fitz Lee on his rear. A number of stragglers had joined him throughout the ride around both the Confederates and the Union army, and he reported a count of 684 troopers and nineteen officers.

"Go get some food and some rest, and have your people do the same. War can be a very unpredictable thing, and what happened to you could have happened to anyone. I will have to initiate an investigation, of course, so be back here at evening meal call and we can discuss the affair in more detail over supper."

As Merritt departed, a trooper arrived, bearing orders for Buford and his division to be ready to ride when relieved by a division of Second Corps. Like Fitz Lee, Buford much preferred the duties of a cavalryman over the static (to him) role of the infantry, so he was pleased to know that he would soon be back in the saddle and on the move. At the same time, he hoped there would be sufficient time for Merritt and his troopers to rest before they had to mount up. He had been considering incorporating the now greatly reduced Reserve Brigade into the First and Second Brigades, but he now decided to keep them a separate unit under the command of Merritt. They would be useful as a scouting force.

Buford began issuing orders for the move, sending staff officers scurrying to inform Colonels Gamble and Devin of the impending move. Buford then turned to Captain Charles Norris, a West Pointer and career cavalry officer who enjoyed Buford's trust and confidence.

"Charlie, go check with your friends on Pleasonton's staff, and see if you can find out what we will be doing once we are relieved here "

It always helped to be a step ahead of things.

* * *

The rain continued its incessant drenching downpour. The interior of Lee's tent was dripping so badly that Lee was forced to accept the hospitality of the hotel in Williamsport that faced the square in the center of town. He could now work out a plan of action without the annoying distraction of dripping cold water. The three corps commanders, as well as Stuart and Lieutenant Colonel Porter Alexander, Longstreet's trusted artillery officer, present at Longstreet's request, were assembled in the dining room.

Lee entered, followed by his aide, Taylor, carrying a large map that he spread on a table.

"Gentlemen, there's no need for me to dwell on the gravity of our situation, which I am sure you all apprehend. We must assume that the rumors of the movement of an additional corps from Grant's army are true and that they could arrive two or three days from now, increasing the need to act as soon as we can to break through Meade's lines. Here I must acknowledge that I under-estimated Meade's abilities and have let him steal the initiative, but I intend to reverse that. With the aid of the weather, Meade has taken the initiative and obviously intends to lay siege until we surrender. To avoid that, we will break out and return to Virginia."

Pointing to the map, Lee continued. "The weakest points in the Union line are where they anchor on the river. We will make a night attack on each simultaneously, First Corps at the south point, Second Corps at the north, Third Corps in reserve. Pioneers have been stripping every barn and warehouse of planks to build pontoons for crossing the river. Once break out its achieved, each corps must rapidly proceed to the crossing located by your engineers. Third Corps will provide rear guard for both break out attacks. I want artillery to be manned and ready to take under fire any attempt to contest the breakout. If the rains hold off the river should have receded enough to permit fording at Williamsport by midnight tomorrow evening. If the river is still too high, we will still break out at midnight tomorrow evening but only at the southern end, in which case, General Ewell and the Second Corps will man the lines until Third and First Corps have cleared. And we will not cross at Falling Waters; instead, we will push on until we have a suitable place far enough downstream to get us behind Howard and Parke.

"I'm sure it is clear to all that we must move quickly and quietly. The risk we are taking is indeed high, but the interdiction of our resupply from Winchester has placed us in a near-desperate situation, given our low level of ammunition, and desperate situations call for desperate measures. I have full confidence that this army will perform at the highest level possible, and with the grace of the Almighty, we will prevail."

As he finished speaking, Lee fixed his gaze on Ewell, unnoticed by Hill and Longstreet. Ewell looked down for a moment, then raising his head, he met Lee's gaze, nodded and left

To the northwest, heavy dark storm clouds were gathering in the mountains.

* * *

Longstreet returned to his corps headquarters and summoned his division commanders. After informing them of Lee's plan, he asked if there were any questions or comments.

"Yes, sir." It was Brigadier General Evander Law, commanding Hood's Division in place of the wounded Hood. "As you know, there are three Texas regiments in my division, and a number of them have spent some time fighting the Comanches. I've heard them say that they have found the best way to fight the Comanches is to use the stealthy, unexpected Comanche-style tactics, and it occurred to me that if we use our 'Comanches' to silently take out the pickets, we could slip out and be on our way before the Yanks become aware of it."

Longstreet stared at Law, who began to think that he had made a mistake by suggesting such an unconventional tactic, especially since he and Longstreet did not get along very well. Then Longstreet spoke.

"By Jehovah almighty, I think it might work! Round up those Texans and send them here but do so quietly."

A half hour later, twenty-six Texans, led by Sergeant Ben England, entered Longstreet's tent, crowding together as they faced their corps commander.

"Sergeant, I understand that you all are Comanche-style fighters. Is that correct?"

"Yes, sir, we've learned their way of fightin', and have used it against them."

Longstreet described Lee's plan, and then asked them if they thought they could use their Comanche tactics to take out the pickets at either end without being discovered.

"Well, Gen'ral, there is always the risk of somethin'' messin' up, but it's worth a try, and if we're found out, ain't no different than if we hadn't tried, but I'd say the odds are in our favor." A murmur of assent arose from the other Texans.

"Tell me how you would do this."

"Well, sir, first off, we'd wear our buckskins 'cause they don't make any sound and don't bind your movement, and we'd blacken all exposed skin. We'd also have observed the routine of the pickets so we would understand who goes where and when. I would let the pickets change before hittin' them since they probably stand picket duty for at least two hours. Then we go in and down them one by one. Shouldn't take longer than thirty minutes, probably less. When we're done, we'll send our best runners to inform you."

Longstreet stood up, thanked them, and after cautioning them to keep the discussion strictly to themselves, dismissed them. His next move was to visit General Lee.

* * *

Major General John Parke, West Point class of 1849, was four months senior by date of rank to Howard, but readily acceded to having Howard continue as overall commander of the blocking forces across the river from Williamsport, given Howard's knowledge of the intentions of General Meade as well as his familiarity with the area. Nevertheless, he felt the need to personally apprise himself of the details of the plan and the tactical situation facing his Ninth Corps.

Howard had requested that the Ninth take over the Falling Waters sector, and it was there that Parke, and his staff were inspecting the emplacement of artillery and infantry fortifications. Gazing across the river, Parke asked himself where he would choose to cross if he were Lee. A member of Howard's staff, Captain Nelson, had been assigned to Parke's staff as liaison with Howard, and it was he that Parke now questioned.

"Captain, are there additional fords and ferries farther downstream that could be used by Lee?"

"Sir, the next one that I know of is at Shepherdstown, but I would expect that there are others between here and there."

Parke nodded, making a mental note to place mounted sentries at intervals of a half-mile along the river down to Shepherdstown. He also intended to have his engineers check for likely locations that might be used to cross either by fording or pontoon bridge.

Considering the difficulty Lee would have in trying to cross against entrenched forces, he doubted that Lee would make such a move. It was more likely that he would try crossing at a spot that was not defended or only lightly so. While Parke recognized the need to entrench opposite Williamsport and at Falling Waters, he thought that a rapidly deployable force should be ready to move quickly to wherever Lee might try to cross, should Lee first be able to break through Meade's lines. And, of course, the weather and the river would be important factors as to when Lee would make his move.

Mounted Federal picket on the Potomac.
iStock.com

After thoroughly viewing the lay of the land, he ordered his headquarters tent to be set up at Falling Waters, where he then began organizing his forces in anticipation of an attempted crossing in his sector. He made note of the need to discuss his intentions with Howard, and Meade as well, if Howard agreed with Parke's preparations.

There was much to be done and not much time in which to do it. And the rain continued.

* * *

Captain Norris tethered his horse to a nearby tree branch and entered Pleasonton's headquarters tent. Spotting his friend and West Point classmate, Norris walked over to the map table where Frank was working.

Norris quietly said, "Excuse me, Captain."

Looking up, Frank smiled when he saw it was Norris who had interrupted his work.

"Charlie, what brings you here?"

"General Buford would like to know what the next assignment will be. You know how he always wants to plan well ahead, so if you can give me that information, I'd be much obliged."

"Sure, Charlie. In fact, that's the task I'm working on now, the orders for Buford and Kilpatrick. It's the usual routine of patrol and being alert to inform Meade of any apparent major move by the enemy. In addition, Buford is tasked with checking the river between here and Shepherdstown for ferries, any such to be destroyed when found. That latter task has highest priority and is to be accomplished as rapidly as possible. Any news for me that we should know?"

"Well, several hundred more stragglers from Merritt's brigade have made it back, so he now has almost 900 troopers and all but two of his officers. Buford intends to use him as a special scouting force. Nothing else. Thanks for your information, much appreciate it. "

As Norris was riding back to Buford's headquarters, he was mentally searching for the right reasoning that would persuade Buford to let him lead the group that would destroy the ferries. He enjoyed serving under Buford, but he nevertheless itched to get out into the field where, before the war, he had spent many a day tracking fugitive, or dealing with the native Indians, and he missed the more active life of a cavalryman in the saddle. He especially wanted to get into some action in the field and saw the ferry tasking as a means to do so. Norris was beginning to feel excitement at the prospect of once again leading cavalrymen in action. If only this blasted rain would stop.

* * *

Lee was thinking the same thing: if only this rain would stop. Bowing his head, he whispered, "Heavenly Father, hear my plea for respite from this rain. You know the depth of my concern for these brave men who have suffered so much for the cause of Southern independence. Grant them Thy merciful compassion and help us find a way to get them to Virginia. In Jesus' name I pray. Amen."

Longstreet had arrived as Lee was praying, and was standing just inside the tent flap, hat in hand, and echoing Lee, Longstreet whispered, "Amen."

Lee looked up, and with a weary smile, said. "Ah, it's my old warhorse. Please come in and tell me what's on your mind."

"Sir, I heard you praying for a way to break out of here, and I may have the answer to your prayer."

Longstreet proceeded to describe the details of the plan to use the "Comanche" Texans. Lee sat deep in thought, mentally analyzing what Longstreet had told him. Finally, Lee spoke.

"I am reluctant to adopt that kind of warfare, but in view of our situation, I see no better alternative, so you have my permission to use the Texans. When you have worked out the plan with Hill and Ewell, I wish for the three of you to meet with me here.

"There is another problem I have been wrestling with, and that is the question of the 4,000 prisoners we have. I have concluded that they, like the wagons and the wounded, must be left behind. Inform Pickett and direct him to hold the prisoners under guard until we have effected the breach at your end, at which time he should join up with you. The prisoners must not learn of this for obvious reasons."

Longstreet studied the ground for a moment, then said, "General, if I may, I suggest that we release the prisoners, sending them, without escort, under a flag of truce. We will simply tell them they are being released because we see no way to safely transport them across the river under these conditions, and we do not wish to wantonly endanger them. I expect they will be only too willing to rejoin their people. We should do this without first telling the Yanks, because they will refuse to accept them, but if the prisoners suddenly appear, marching across to their lines, Meade will be unable to refuse them."

"When do you propose doing this?"

"Tomorrow afternoon, sir."

Longstreet's proposal made sense: it would clear away a potential risk of the prisoners causing a disruption of the breakout once they became aware of it, as well as solve the problem of feeding and guarding them while hiding from them any preparations for breaking out. There was the risk that releasing the prisoners would alert Meade that something was afoot, but the benefits outweighed the risk, especially if the breakout was done before Meade could make any meaningful preparations.

"Thank you, Pete; make it so. We must make our move no later than tomorrow at midnight."

* * *

Meade read again the message sent from Grant, advising Lincoln, Stanton, Halleck and Meade that he was about to depart Cincinnati and expected to arrive at the "agreed destination" tomorrow evening. Following the meeting with the "man from Illinois," he requested a briefing on the situation in the East. A message from Halleck had arrived, requesting that Meade send his chief of staff to the meeting in order to brief Grant. Warren, who had been the temporary chief of staff, had been relieved by Brigadier General Andrew Humphreys, previously commanding Second Division, Third Corps. Humphreys was standing nearby, having been summoned by Meade. He had read the messages and was waiting for Meade to speak.

"I assume General Halleck will give the briefing to General Grant, even though he requested that you do it. That's just his way. If so, note anything that needs correcting, and inform Grant after you leave the meeting. A special train will take you from Frederick as soon as you arrive. It will wait for you in Baltimore to bring you back as soon as you are able to leave. Offer in my name to bring Grant here with you. If he doesn't come with you, be sure to ask him when we can expect Ord to arrive. Questions?"

"No, sir."

As Humphreys departed, Meade was wondering if Grant would take Halleck's place as general-in-chief and, if so, how that would affect the conduct of the war. Then his mind returned to the current situation and how to anticipate Lee's next move. Clearly, Lee could not afford to just sit and do nothing; he had to attempt to break the siege, but when, and how?

He had considered calling a meeting with the corps commanders, but after further reflection, he had rejected the idea. It was time that decisions were made by the commanding general; an army could not be led successfully by a committee.

"Excuse me, sir." It was a young lieutenant from his staff. "General Parke has arrived. "

After exchanging greetings, Parke set about explaining the steps he had taken to prepare for a possible crossing attempt by Lee.

"Sir, I have stationed pickets along the Potomac between Falling Waters and Shepherdstown at intervals of a half-mile with instructions to fire three quick shots upon sighting any attempt to cross or if sighted moving toward Shepherdstown, and to be especially alert at night. Each picket upstream from the alerting picket will fire also, thereby sending a rapid alert to our base at Martinsburg. I will then move a ready division as quickly as possible to oppose the crossing, with the remainder of the corps following. Each of my three divisions will serve as the ready division every third day. The ready division will be on standby for the full twenty-four hours, ready to move out within five minutes of being alerted. I hope this meets with your approval, sir."

"It does, indeed, General. Has General Howard made similar arrangements?"

"Yes, sir, he has."

"Good. I expect General Lee to make his move soon, and your preparations are timely."

As Parke departed for the train at Frederick that would return him to his corps, Meade returned to his study of the map showing the disposition of his

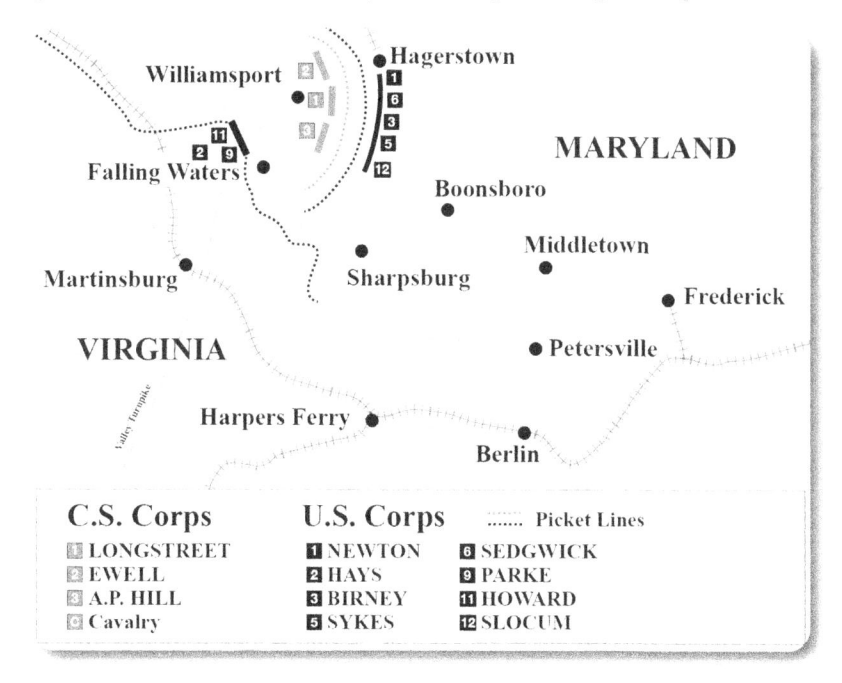

C.S. Corps
1 LONGSTREET
2 EWELL
3 A.P. HILL
4 Cavalry

U.S. Corps
1 NEWTON
2 HAYS
3 BIRNEY
5 SYKES
6 SEDGWICK
9 PARKE
11 HOWARD
12 SLOCUM

.... Picket Lines

Lee under siege
©David John Murphy

forces, while trying to see them as Lee did. Where and when would he, Meade, strike if he were Lee? Parke had instructed his pickets to be especially alert at night. Made sense. Why hadn't he thought of that, or anyone else among his generals? At any rate, he would issue an order to that effect tomorrow.

In the meantime, he decided to list the possible options open to Lee and the measures necessary to thwart each.

If Lee successfully attacked the middle of the Union line, he would have to expose his left flank in order to move toward Baltimore and Washington, the move Meade expected Lee to make since it would force Meade to interpose his army between Lee and the two cities, giving Lee access to a number of fords and ferries downstream. With Lee's flank exposed, however, Meade could hit him a blow that would compel Lee to turn and fight, giving Meade the opportunity to slide around Lee and block any advance toward Washington while also inflicting more losses in the Confederate army. Meade concluded that Lee would see the same scenario and thus would not attack the center.

Attacking either the left or the right of the Union line reduced the exposure of Lee's flank, and if Lee attacked at the Falling Waters area and broke through, he would be able to quickly secure his flank by swinging a division or two to defend his army as it moved toward Washington while also gaining access to fords and ferries. Or he could even leave several divisions in the fortified line the Confederates had erected but doing so essentially conceded the loss of those divisions. Nevertheless, if it meant keeping the remainder of his army relatively intact and enabled their escape to Virginia, it would be worth doing so. Meade concluded that Lee would attack the left flank. It did not occur to him that Lee might attack both flanks simultaneously.

* * *

It was nearing sunset at Cincinnati when the last troops boarded the train that would take them to Baltimore and then to Martinsburg in what was now called West Virginia, although the Confederacy still claimed it as part of Virginia.

None of them noticed the civilian leaning against a tree next to the station where they were boarding the train. Even if they had, he appeared to be somewhat inebriated and half asleep. He was very alert, listening to the chatter of the troops from the West, as they commented about the surroundings. Then he heard one wondering about conditions at Martinsburg, and hoping they were better than Vicksburg, which drew several remarks and guffaws, but one remark captured the civilian's attention. "You'll find out when we arrive there tomorrow evening."

Harrison, Longstreet's one-man intelligence unit, eased upright and slouched away, moving in a wide circle around the station, until he was opposite the telegraph operator's office, some twenty yards or so away. Seeing Harrison, the operator lifted his green visor, and then placed it back on. Approaching the window, Harrison spoke briefly to the operator, and then slipped away. Within twelve hours, Longstreet would know that Ord's corps would be arriving about five pm on July 8.

* * *

It was late in the afternoon when the train bearing President Lincoln, Secretary of War Stanton, Secretary of the Navy Welles and Major General Halleck arrived at the Camden station in Baltimore.

The train was well guarded by a regiment of Union troops and included seven cars, all of which had shaded windows. Lincoln and his entourage occupied the fifth car, and squads of Marines filled the other cars.

After a wait of a half hour or so the Pratt Street trolley carrying Grant arrived at the Howard Street corner, and several nondescript Union officers emerged, their rank insignia hidden underneath the rain ponchos they were wearing. Crossing the street, they entered the station and walked out to the train of cars sitting on a siding. The officer leading the way knocked on the door of the last car. The Marine officer who opened the door escorted them through to the fifth car, where they were first greeted by Halleck, then by the president and the secretaries.

"General Grant, Admiral Porter, let me first congratulate you and offer the heartfelt thanks of a grateful nation for your victory at Vicksburg. Your success, together with Gettysburg, has strengthened our hopes for ending this war soon. I would welcome any advice toward that end from you both."

Grant was struck by the appearance of his commander-in-chief. He had pictured Lincoln as a tall, slightly unkempt man, and so he was, but his eyes conveyed a strength of character that impressed Grant.

Grant spoke first. "Mr. President, first may I say that the capture of Vicksburg would not have been possible without the full cooperation and support we received from the Navy, for which I will forever be grateful to Admiral Porter. As for the situation with Lee, I would ask that I may hold any comments until I have learned the details."

Lincoln nodded and turned to Porter, who expressed his praise of Grant and then indicated he had no further comments.

Lincoln sat down and eased back in his chair. He then turned the focus of the meeting to a report on the details of the fall of Vicksburg, stating that he would not keep them longer than a half hour.

True to his word, thirty minutes later, Lincoln said he had no more questions, thanked Grant and Porter. Accompanied by Halleck, they donned their rain ponchos and left. Porter and Grant shook hands, and Porter departed.

With Halleck leading, Grant entered the yard superintendent's office, where they found Humphreys waiting for them. After introductions, Halleck proceeded to describe, in brief terms, the situation at Williamsport as he understood it. Humphreys listened closely and made a mental note to inform Grant in much greater detail. When Halleck finished, he asked if Grant had any questions.

Grant stood up, took a cigar out of his coat pocket, walked over to the superintendent's desk to the cigar cutter on the desk, cut off the end, lit the cigar, puffed several times, filling the office with smoke, and then turned to face Halleck.

"No, General, thank you." Grant then walked out, followed by Humphreys, leaving a frowning Halleck staring at the door. He was tempted to send a letter of reprimand to Grant; after all, he was still the general-in-chief and deserved the respect of subordinates, but his better judgment prevailed, and he discarded the idea. Although he hated to admit it, he knew, or rather sensed, that his days as general-in-chief were soon to end. He was not a happy warrior.

Grant waited for Humphreys to join him, and they made their way to the special train sitting on a siding for the trip to Frederick, and then to

Meade's headquarters. Once aboard, Humphreys began filling in the details, explaining that Parke and the Ninth Corps were now on the Virginia side with pickets every half-mile between Falling Waters and Shepherdstown.

"What about the section between Williamsport and Cumberland?" Grant asked.

"Howard has placed pickets between Williamsport and Hancock. The bridge at Hancock has been heavily damaged and is considered impassable at present. Nevertheless, Howard has twelve guns opposite Hancock to oppose any attempt to repair it."

"What do we know about the condition of Lee's army?"

"A deserter from Johnson's Division, Ewell's Second Corps, an artilleryman, said that his division had ammunition sufficient for one day of combat, and it's likely that the rest of the army has a similar amount. Howard intercepted and destroyed a resupply effort several days ago, and there have been no additional attempts since then. Obviously, the quartermaster at Winchester knows that we have interdicted the route from Winchester."

"How is Richmond reacting to Lee's situation?"

Humphreys paused, glanced around to see if anyone was within earshot, and then answered. "We have a man in Richmond who sends us by covert means a supply of the Richmond newspapers, as well as any rumors he hears. The papers are as bad as ours in providing information for any and all to read, and according to the news two days ago, Davis has ordered Joe Johnston to bring his army from Mississippi by rail to attempt a relief of Lee. I'm sorry that I don't have more recent information, General."

Grant was silent for several minutes as he digested what he had been told. He tossed the stub of his cigar into a nearby spittoon, removed a fresh cigar from his vest pocket, bit off the end and striking a match, lit the cigar, all the while staring into space as his mind worked on the situation.

"Lee is faced with a very difficult problem. I don't see how he can afford to wait for Johnston to rescue him, and probably doesn't even know that Johnston has been so ordered. He must somehow figure how to get through Meade's line and then get across the river. By now, he should have identified where every Union division is located and should have an estimate of each division's strength. He should also know where ferries are located because he can't ford across until the river goes down. So, he has to use a ferry, or a strong pontoon bridge."

"Sir, he had a pontoon bridge at Falling Waters, but our cavalry from Frederick destroyed it."

Grant's eyebrows raised. "Didn't he have it guarded?"

"Not really, sir. Just a handful of Rebels were there, according to the report from Frederick."

Grant was considering the possible implications of what he had been told when the train, which had started to pull out of the station, slowed and stopped. As Grant and Humphreys stood to see the cause of the stop, the car door opened, and a major climbed up the step. Saluting, he informed Grant that he was to proceed to Washington for a meeting at the White House.

Humphreys departed, and as the train once again began rolling, this time to Washington, Grant began thinking about the prospect of Johnston arriving to unite his Army of the Tennessee with the Army of Northern Virginia. He decided to send a message to Sherman, to advise him to keep a close hold on Johnston and prevent him from coming east.

He noticed that the rain seemed to be slackening. It was an hour before sunset.

* * *

Sergeant England had been observing the Union pickets all day, making notes of their procedures, the number of pickets, their location, and so on. Now he was reviewing his notes while he waited for the Texans who would comprise his special force.

The tent flap parted, and the tent filled with the lean, bronzed Texans he had selected, twenty men he knew he could depend upon to do their task quickly, quietly, and efficiently.

"Alright, boys, make yourselves comfortable, but not too comfortable. What I have to say I am sayin' once and once only, so listen up."

He waited while they arranged themselves, some squatting on the ground, others standing. All looked at him expectantly.

"I've spent the day watchin' them Union pickets, and it's clear they are veteran soldiers. They were all business, no messin' around, and they appeared to be alert the whole time they were on picket. So it ain't gonna be no cake walk, takin' them out. Ever' one of us is gonna have to be damn sure of what you're doin', and how you're gonna take 'em out. Tomorra, borrow some field glasses and study your areas so you know where cover is if needed, and the probable location of your target. Plan what route you're gonna take and rehearse it in your mind so there ain't no hesitation or doubt in your mind about your task. Does every man have a Bowie knife or equivalent?"

All did, and England continued. "We will assemble here at my call tomorra' night, probably about an hour or so before midnight. At that time, we will review our night calls, change into our buckskins, and darken up. In the meantime, no talkin' about this with anybody outside of this group. Any questions? Good. Dismissed."

As they silently departed, England felt a surge of pride in his fellow Texans, men who believed in themselves and one another. At the same time, he could not stop wishing that their killing mission could somehow be aborted. He did not relish the idea of taking the lives of the Yanks in this manner, but he would do his duty as ordered.

* * *

Captain Norris was beginning to regret having volunteered to lead the group charged with destroying every ferry in Maryland between Falling Waters and Shepherdstown. Irate citizens were visibly upset and loudly complaining. How were they to get their goods to market across the river? Aunt Sarah was depending on nephew Hiram to bring her much needed staples, so, mister soldier, how can I get them to her now? And on and on, at every ferry. The ferry operators were not happy either about their loss of revenue and the cost of replacing their equipment. Norris took the names of the ferry operators, promising them that the government would reimburse them but neither he nor they really believed that.

Norris tried explaining the reason for what his men were doing, and while some seemed to understand what was at stake, others either were not sympathetic to the Union cause, or simply resented anything that interfered with their lives. It was they who so strongly objected and threatened Norris and his men.

Because of having to deal with the objectors, Norris did not notice that one of the civilians seemed to appear at every ferry location. But one of his troopers remarked to the sergeant that he had noticed "that feller over there by the big oak was at every ferry." The trooper nodded his head in the direction of the civilian, who then quickly moved away.

Harrison realized he had been spotted and used the crowd of objectors to conceal his retrieval of his horse. He rode downstream and then swerved quickly left into thick woods where he stopped and listened for any pursuers. All was silent, so he continued through the woods, emerging on the north side, where he again stopped and listened. This time he heard what he took to be the noise of horses trotting on the road on the other side of the woods. He turned his horse back into the woods where he dismounted and moved the horse behind several thick laurel bushes, holding the bridle to keep his horse still.

Norris and three troopers saw where Harrison had disturbed the ground that was soft from the rain and followed the track through the woods. Harrison realized his mistake, and cursing to himself, decided to make a run. Mounting his horse, he spurred out of the woods at a full gallop.

The first trooper to emerge saw Harrison bent low, riding hard and rapidly opening the distance. Raising his carbine, the trooper took careful aim at the horse's hind quarters and fired three rounds, hitting the horse, causing it to stumble and then fall, tossing Harrison to the ground.

Stunned by the fall, Harrison tried to stand but fell back to the ground. He was trying again to stand when he heard Norris say, "Don't move!" Then he felt two troopers pulling him upright, followed by one of them twisting his arms behind him while the other bound his wrists together.

Scribbling a quick note describing what had occurred, Norris directed the troopers to take Harrison to the provost marshal. Captain Charles Norris did not realize the value of capturing Harrison. Longstreet had lost his one-man intelligence unit.

* * *

Brigadier General Henry Hunt happily greeted the Navy captain and the several hundred sailors and Marines who had accompanied the twelve large mortars on the trip from the Washington Navy Yard. Each mortar had a twelve-man gun crew who were well trained in the details of firing these monsters. Weighing some 900 pounds, each mortar was secured to a strong metal ring resting on a square plate. The ring allowed the mortar to rotate

360 degrees, while a sturdy wooden quoin was used to adjust the angle of elevation. The mortars could hurl a twelve-inch 200-pound projectile about two miles in a high arching trajectory that made the rounds seem to fall out of the sky. Loaded with canister and fused to explode above the target, the deadly spray of the canister balls made them a fearsome weapon. It was Hunt's intention to hit the Confederates continually in a slow and irregular rate of fire that was intended to wear down the unfortunate recipients of these most unwelcome visitors.Hunt and Captain Freeman, USN, quickly directed the offloading and placement of the mortars. Within three hours, Hunt reported to Meade that the mortars were in place behind well-constructed revetments and the first section of four guns was manned and ready to commence firing.

With Meade's approval, the four mortars began firing, the arrival of the high arching shells being noted by observers who called out corrections for the line of sight and the angle of elevation. The targets selected were all artillery sites, and as the observers walked the rounds toward the targets, they saw the Confederate gun crews bringing up teams of horses to move the guns and any ready ammunition there. The Union crews were told to change to canister, and when those rounds burst overhead, the resultant carnage was horrendous. Men and horses were cut into bloody pieces that showered upon those who were not hit, creating panic among the veteran troops.

Siege mortars employed by Federals.
iStock.com

* * *

Longstreet and Porter Alexander had been inspecting the artillery emplacements when the mortar rounds started to fall. Now they witnessed the carnage caused and the effect it was having on the troops.

Disregarding the danger, Alexander spurred his mount forward, shouting for the gunners to evacuate and take cover.

There was a short pause in the bombardment as the Union gunners changed to solid shot. Just as the Confederates were considering returning to their guns, a large ball of iron came hurtling out of the sky, falling just short of the revetment. Other rounds came in at irregular intervals, methodically destroying the two cannons in the revetment as well as the revetment itself.

Longstreet waited for Alexander to work out in his thinking how he thought the Confederates could counter this new and unforeseen threat.

After a few moments, Alexander shook his head and said, "There is no way our guns can match the destructive power of those mortars. We can try to run a gun up an incline to give it more elevation but unless we use a dangerous amount of powder that might burst the gun, our rounds will not have enough range to reach their mortars when fired at such a high elevation of the muzzle. If we want to save our guns, we'll have to move them back out of range of their mortars. As I recall, their maximum range is about two miles, so we will have to move the guns back about half a mile. The infantry will have to stay where they are now, so they had better start digging out some deep bomb shelters."

Longstreet nodded and rode off to inform Lee. The need to break out tomorrow night had increased significantly.

* * *

Over on the Union side, Meade had joined Hunt and Freeman to observe the effect of the mortars and was clearly impressed.

"Whose idea was it to use these mortars? Was it yours, Henry?" Meade asked.

"I wish I could claim it was, sir, but actually it was Admiral Porter who suggested that they might be useful as harassment weapons. I don't think even he realized their destructive power. Porter made the suggestion to General Halleck, who contacted me, and Captain Freeman and I worked out the details."

Hunt then congratulated Freeman on the excellent performance of his gunners, echoed by Meade as well. Some of the sailors overheard the conversation and quickly passed it on to the rest of their mates. With a rousing cheer, the sailors and Marines resumed their torment of the Confederates, a torment that would continue round the clock.

* * *

Lee received Longstreet's report with his usual equanimity, a never-ending source of wonderment to Longstreet. How could any man in Lee's situation receive such news and remain calm and even thoughtful?

"Pete, tell Alexander to leave the guns where they are. If those people concentrate their fire on destroying our artillery, it will mean less rounds fired against our troops. If we manage to break out without being discovered, we will have to abandon the guns anyway. But that does not apply to Ewell's corps."

Ignoring Longstreet's puzzled look, Lee then added that he wished to receive the details of the breakout plan at noon tomorrow.

With Jackson gone, it was apparent that Lee relied even more upon Longstreet to get things done. Lee had never given Jackson more than the idea of his intentions, yet Lee and Jackson were so attuned to the other's thinking, Jackson knew exactly what to do. Longstreet, on the other hand, never felt comfortable or confident that he was carrying out the old man's intentions, despite Lee's obvious trust in him.

Night was approaching and much remained to be done as Longstreet returned to his headquarters while Lee, the ache in his left arm nagging him ceaselessly, turned in for some badly needed rest.

* * *

In January 1863, a group of Confederate cavalry officers, led by Major General J. E. B. Stuart, met in a small farmhouse at Rector's Crossroads in Loudon County, northern Virginia. It was at that meeting that Captain John Singleton Mosby persuaded Stuart to approve Mosby's request to form an independent band of partisan rangers under Mosby's command.

Within several months, Mosby's rangers, less than two hundred in number, had established a reputation for daring and fearlessness by means of swift strikes at night, capturing horses, equipment, and other goods, as well as taking prisoners, including a sleeping brigadier general and 58 of his command.

The rangers, who were farmers by day and marauders in the night, would prove to be a real problem for the Union forces in northern Virginia and eventually incurred the wrath of the Union general in charge of the Valley, who, at one point, ordered any rangers that might be captured to be summarily hanged as thieves, an order that was rescinded when Mosby responded in kind with captured Union soldiers.

On June 10, 1863, Mosby was promoted to the rank of major. He aided Stuart in late June as Stuart and his cavalry swept through northern Virginia on their way to Gettysburg.

When Mosby learned of Lee's defeat at Gettysburg, followed by the loss of Vicksburg, he determined to conduct a reprisal raid consisting of tearing up as much track of the Baltimore and Ohio Railroad as could be done during the hours of darkness. He selected a stretch of track that ran through Howard County, Maryland, and he and 74 of his rangers assembled in the designated area, coming in one by one to avoid being noticed.

By the time dawn was beginning to break, they had loosened the rails at various intervals over almost ten miles of track, leaving the rails sitting in place but loosened sufficiently to cause the derailment of a train. Their work done, the rangers quietly and singly departed, being careful to avoid any patrols that might be about. This was done during the night of July 7-8.

As he rode back to the house near Rectortown, Virginia, where he was staying, it occurred to Mosby that no trains had appeared during their foray, a circumstance that was unusual to Mosby, who had several times raided trains on that stretch of track during the night hours.

* * *

Major General Edward Ord sat fuming in the railroad car attached to the train that he had boarded at Cincinnati. They had been sitting on the west side of the Susquehanna River for over an hour while the railroad people and their civil engineers worked on shoring up the railroad bridge that was threatened by the flooded river as the floodwaters rushed past. The relentless pounding of the river, together with additional pounding from heavy large trees and other debris being swept down the river, had caused the railroad to halt all crossings until they could be sure of a safe crossing. The rail line to Baltimore that ran west of the Susquehanna could not be used due to reports of Confederate forces being seen in the area through which the line passed. However, Ord was rapidly losing patience and was considering ordering the trains to proceed by that route.

At sunset, darkness had quickly enveloped the land under the heavy downpour. Now, the rain seemed to be slackening, the drum of it on the roof of the rail car was gradually becoming quieter, but the noise of the river's rushing water seemed just as loud as ever.

Sliding a rubber poncho over his head and onto his shoulders, Ord opened the car door and stepped down onto the soggy ground. Carefully making his way alongside the car, he approached the engineers who were studying a blueprint of the bridge.

"Excuse me, gentlemen. I am General Ord, commanding the troops you are taking to join General Meade. I was wondering if you could give me an estimate as to when we might be on our way?"

An older man stepped forward and identified himself as the superintendent of this section of the railroad, responsible for the safe operation of the railroad, among other things. He reiterated what Ord already knew about the threat to the bridge from the floodwaters, but then, pausing, he said, "General, I am aware of the exigencies of war and of the urgent need for you to join General Meade. If you are willing to accept the responsibility for any mishap that may occur while crossing the river, your needs will override my concern."

Ord turned to the two civil engineers and asked them what the odds were for a safe passage across the river.

"Fifty-fifty, General," said one, the other nodding in agreement. "If the train's engineer is willing to take you across, and if he avoids any sudden heavy wheel action, you may well make it. If he does agree to go, he should back up a mile or so to get a running start and should maintain a steady speed of fifteen miles per hour to minimize stressing the bridge."

The superintendent fetched the train's engineer, who approached somewhat warily. Ord had already met the engineer who had greeted him in Cincinnati.

After explaining the situation at Gettysburg, and repeating the advice given by the civil engineer, Ord said, "So, Mr. Johnson, will you take us across?"

Impressed by the details given him by a major general, Mr. Johnson's sense of patriotism impelled him to agree with a hearty "Yes, sir!"

With handshakes all around, the group dispersed. The superintendent and the two civil engineers watched as word was sent to the other trains behind as to the need to cross one at a time, and to follow the advice of the civil engineers.

The trains all having backed, Johnson started forward, and was coming on at fifteen miles per hour. As the train rode out onto the bridge, Johnson felt a slight tremor, and for several seconds, he held his breath, waiting to see what might happen, all the while carefully maintaining a steady, smooth speed. Other than an occasional sway, the rest of the crossing was uneventful.

Half an hour later, the trains pulled into the station at Harrisburg, where Ord was met by the governor and the mayor, who insisted that the troops be given the word to debark for a hot meal awaiting them. Ord reluctantly did so, but when he saw the eager reaction of both officers and men, he realized that his men had been away from any friendly people, as well as a home-cooked hot meal, for months, and his corps would be in much better shape when they once again entered the combat zone as the result of a few hours break and some good hot food.

A group of reporters from various area newspapers were present, and Ord asked them to convey the deep gratitude of the Thirteenth Corps as well as his personal thanks to "the good people of Harrisburg for their splendid and thoughtful support" of his soldiers.

It would be another four hours before their trains would depart Harrisburg for Baltimore. He dutifully reported the situation to Meade, including an estimated arrival in Baltimore at 0600. The track between Harrisburg and Baltimore had been cleared for several hours and would remain so until Ord's corps arrived at Baltimore, so Ord was expecting no further delays and was looking forward to completing the long trip from Vicksburg.

Ord's message to Meade arrived well before midnight, mixed in with a number of routine reports, all of which required decoding. The young staff officer who received them from the telegrapher quickly scanned the senders and just as quickly concluded that they were routine reports that could wait until tomorrow to be decoded. In his haste, he missed noting the one message that was not routine, and so Ord's message remained unseen.

* * *

Lee was having a restless night. He had gone to bed early in anticipation of the attempt tomorrow night to break through the Union siege line. He had discussed the plan with his corps commanders after they had briefed him on their proposal. Hood's Comanches would take out the pickets at each end of the line, being careful to avoid being discovered, that being top priority; surprise was critical for the success of their plan. Once Sergeant England reported to Longstreet, he would send couriers to Hill and Ewell, informing them of the time to simultaneously begin the breakout, with Hill hitting the southern end of the line and Ewell moving on the north end. The decision as to which end for Longstreet's corps to take would depend upon the situation as it developed. That decision would be made by General Lee.

In addition to the questions about details that kept coming to mind, Lee's left arm ached, regardless of any position he took, causing him to toss and turn. Finally, shortly before midnight, Lee drifted into a fitful sleep, his weary body at last dominating his restless mind.

* * *

Ord was enjoying his dinner with the governor and the mayor of Harrisburg at the governor's home when he heard the clock in the hall striking the hour of eleven. Citing the need to get his corps back on the trains in order to arrive in Baltimore in the morning, Ord thanked his hosts and mounting his horse, headed to the large hall in the center of town where his corps officers were dining. Although his division commanders had been invited to dine with the governor, they had demurred, preferring to remain with their officers. They were not sure how their men would react to being the center of attention among the many young women who had volunteered to help with the cooking and serving chores. The generals were banking on their presence to maintain order.

When Ord arrived at the hall, he found that his division commanders were already gathering the men from the several locations where they had dined. There had been no problems, the older veterans having kept the young bucks in line, and the troops were quietly assembling with their companies. For many, being with civilians who treated them as if they were family, the memories of the homes they had left came so strongly, the effect was sobering, especially now as they considered that the morrow would find them back in combat.

The trains slowly moved out of the station, with their civilian hosts waving and wishing them well. As the trains disappeared, the telegrapher began receiving a message from Baltimore, stating that a cavalry patrol had captured one of Mosby's men who bragged to them that the Baltimore and Ohio Railroad would soon be out of business. A patrol had set out from Fairfax a few minutes ago to check the rail line between Baltimore and Frederick, according to the message, and had requested that a patrol be sent out of Frederick to check between Frederick and Harrisburg. In the meantime, the message recommended alerting General Ord.

The telegrapher made a copy for the file and knowing that there was no telegraph station between Baltimore and his station, he shrugged his shoulders and concluded there was nothing more he could do. Besides, it was late, and he was tired and sleepy.

* * *

Ord was dozing in his seat on the lead car of the lead train when he was awakened by the sound of the brakes slowing the train to a complete stop. Ord left the car and saw what appeared to be a Union cavalry patrol, gathered by the cab of the steam engine. Noting Ord's approach, the lieutenant who had been talking with Johnson, the engineer, dismounted, saluted, and greeted Ord.

It was a few minutes before midnight. The rain had stopped, the clouds were rapidly clearing, and a bright full moon was breaking through, dispelling the darkness.

After hearing the lieutenant's explanation as to why he had stopped the train, Ord felt a growing sense of unease, and ordered pickets to be posted, and personal weapons to be readied. He informed his staff and his division commanders to form up at 0400, each man to be issued a full cartridge case, and be ready to march at dawn.

He also wrote a note for delivery to Halleck by the cavalry lieutenant, informing him of the situation and of Ord's intent to march down the rail tracks to where the rails were still intact, with the request that transportation be there for the remaining travel to Baltimore.

When Ord asked at what time the lieutenant estimated his arrival at Washington, he was told it would be in about two hours. Ord thanked the lieutenant and sent him on his way. The off-loading of artillery and cavalry horses, together with the guns and caissons, he ordered to commence at 0200.

As he climbed aboard the car, an officer handed him a cup of coffee, which Ord welcomed as he wearily slumped into his seat. He had the feeling that the coming day was going to be long and difficult.

* * *

Grant had been summoned to the White House just as he was about to board the train that would take him to Frederick. He spent over two hours with President Lincoln and Secretary Stanton., explaining his views on the war and how he thought it should be fought, with emphasis on the destruction of the Army of Northern Virginia.

When asked by Stanton for his opinion of Lee, Grant replied, "I will be honest with you, sir, and tell you that I am tired of hearing our senior officers worrying about what General Lee is going to do next. It's time that we started making him worry about what we may do next."

Lincoln and Stanton exchanged glances. Then Lincoln took his pen and signed the paper that was before him. He handed the paper to Stanton whose signature was already on it. Stanton, in turn handed it to Grant. Initiated by Stanton, the paper sought the approval of the president to replace Halleck with Grant as general-in-chief, in the rank of lieutenant general.

Although Grant had suspected that this might come about, the reality of the enormous responsibility that was now on his shoulders left him speechless. Lincoln and Stanton both rose from the table, and extending his hand, Lincoln warmly congratulated Grant and expressed full confidence in Grant's ability to bring the war to a successful conclusion, and hopefully soon. Grant promised to do just that, a promise made not only to the president but to himself as well.

As Grant and Stanton headed toward Army headquarters across 17th Street, Grant expressed his desire to retain Halleck in Washington as chief of staff to handle the day-to-day administration of the Army, thus enabling Grant to be in the field where he could confront Lee face to face. Stanton agreed, and they entered the building to inform Halleck of the change. Halleck had steeled himself for this moment, but it was obvious to Stanton and Grant that Halleck was shaken.

Stanton gave Halleck a copy of the order for Grant to replace him as general-in-chief, and nodding to each, departed, mentally questioning whether Halleck could be trusted, given his well-known dislike of Grant.

With an attempt at a smile, Halleck congratulated Grant, and started gathering his personal effects.

"Hold on, General, " Grant said. "If you agree, I would much appreciate having you stay as chief of staff of the Army, running the administrative side of things, freeing me to be in the field."

Clearly surprised by Grant's request, Halleck stared at Grant for several seconds, then stammered, "General, I am honored by your offer, which I accept with the promise to do my best in bringing victory to our cause."

After shaking hands, Grant produced two cigars, and as the rich tobacco smoke filled the room, they began working on Grant's plans.

JULY 8, 1863

Lee awoke to the sound of the continuing Union bombardment, and for several seconds, he could not recognize where he was. Then he remembered moving into this room at the small hotel in Williamsport, the leaking of his tent having increased to the point that he could no longer do any work there.

As he arose from the bed, he glanced out the window and noticed that the rain had stopped. His watch showed the time to be 3:43 am, sunrise was at 4:14 am, so he decided to wash and dress, and then have some breakfast.

Walter Taylor softly knocked on the door and hearing Lee's "Enter," went in with a mug of steaming hot coffee. Lee sipped the coffee as Taylor brought him up to date on plans for the day, the principal event being a conference with the corps commanders at noon for a final look at the plan they had devised.

Taylor added that the release of the prisoners was scheduled for 4:30 pm.

"Who has knowledge of this so far?" Lee asked.

"Just you, General Longstreet and I, sir. It is Longstreet's intention to have the prisoners assembled in ranks at about 4:15 pm, and at that time, to inform them of your decision to release them for humanitarian reasons. They will then be placed under the command of a Colonel Watson, the senior officer, and told to proceed through the lines. Longstreet will send an officer under flag of truce to inform the Yankees that we are releasing their people and suggest that they may wish to cease their bombardment until the prisoners have all safely crossed into their lines."

"Pete has been busy," mused Lee.

The sound of a shell exploding rattled the windows, and Lee once more stated the need to break the siege no later than that night. The troops must be kept under shelter until the very last minute tonight to keep any casualties to a minimum. The unpredictable timing of the shelling, the release of the prisoners, the need for the Texans to eliminate the pickets without being detected, and the ever-present tendency in war for unplanned things to happen that caused plans to fail, all weighed on his mind. Taylor had departed, and Lee bowed his head in a silent prayer, ending with "thy will be done. Amen."

* * *

Grant had departed for his hotel room shortly before midnight, and Halleck was completing the draft of the plans that he and Grant had been working on, when a knock on his office door startled him. He had sent the office staff home when Grant left, including the colonel who manned his outer office. The wall clock was showing six minutes past two o'clock.

Halleck opened the door, revealing the sergeant of the guard and a mud-spattered lieutenant of cavalry. Dismissing the sergeant, Halleck invited the young officer to enter.

"Sir, I bear a message from General Ord. I don't know if you are aware of the B & O's rails having been loosened at irregular intervals over a span of almost ten miles in Howard County."

"Yes, I was informed earlier this evening," Halleck replied.

"Well, sir, that has caused all rail traffic to be stopped between Westminster and Baltimore, including the trains bringing the Thirteenth Corps to Baltimore. My patrol fortunately was able to intercept those trains not far from where we had found the northernmost loosening, and stopped them, but Thirteenth Corps is going to be delayed as a result. General Ord is marching his corps down the tracks and has requested that transportation be ready at the southern end of the affected tracks at 0600, and he wanted you and General Meade to know what was happening."

Halleck walked out into the hall, and shouted, "Sergeant of the guard!"

"Yes, sir," he heard, as the sergeant ran up the stairs.

"Sergeant, inform the duty officer that I wish to see him as quickly as he can get here." Turning to the lieutenant, he said, "I have one more task for you, Lieutenant, and that is to go to the Willard Hotel and inform General Grant, who is now the general-in-chief. Tell him that I will pursue the matter of transportation for Ord. I will also send a message to General Meade."

Pausing, Halleck glanced at the lieutenant's insignia and said, "You're Eighth Illinois."

"Yes, sir."

"Is the rest of your patrol with you here?"

"No, sir, I sent them on to Fairfax. They have been in the saddle since this afternoon."

At this point, the duty officer arrived. Addressing him, Halleck said, "Captain, provide the lieutenant an armed escort to the Willard Hotel and then to his outfit at Fairfax. Washington at this hour can be a dangerous city. And then return here to assist me with some messages."

Halleck drafted a message to General Haupt, and another to Meade, informing Haupt of the need for trains for Ord and informing Meade of Ord's delay, marked both Urgent, and handed them to the duty officer for transmission. He then decided that sleep was his next priority, closed the office door, and laid down on the couch in the outer office. He was sleeping soundly within several minutes.

Awakened by someone rapping on the door, Halleck arose, lit the oil lamp on the desk, and opened the door. It was the duty officer.

"Sorry to disturb you, sir, but I thought you would want to see this now."

It was from Haupt. "Regret no trains available until after 1200 this date. Suggest Ord continue march or set up camp at current location. Have found that track bed has been mined at several locations, requiring detailed examination of almost ten miles of tracks to determine if there are other locations mined. Haupt."

Halleck noted that Meade was also in the address. It was now nearing 5 am, and the sun was climbing in the east. The day was already hot and gave every sign that it would grow even hotter in Washington. Halleck donned his uniform jacket, called for his mount, and set out for the Willard Hotel to check with the general-in-chief as to what orders should be given to Ord. He knew that Meade would not be happy to hear this. Grant, however, was an unknown factor, and Halleck was curious as to what his reaction as general-in-chief would be.

When Halleck arrived at the hotel, he found Grant having breakfast in the dining room. Halleck informed him of Haupt's message, and asked if Grant had any orders for Ord.

Offering Halleck a cigar, which Halleck declined, Grant lit his cigar, puffed on it for several minutes, and then spoke.

"Tell Ord to use his best judgment of the situation and let us know his decision. He's on the scene and can make a better decision than I can, sitting here in this hotel. Anything heard from Meade this morning?"

"Not yet, but I expect he will not be happy about Ord's delay."

Grant nodded. Looking up at Halleck who had arisen and was about to depart, Grant said, "General, go home, get a good rest, and come back after a good breakfast tomorrow. Unless I am needed sooner, I will delay my departure until you return. Once I get in the field, you will have enough work to keep you here."

Halleck was uncertain as to whether to be pleased or worried, and after a brief pause, saluted and left. One thing was certain, he knew who was in charge.

* * *

Sergeant England had a good picture of the picket routine after two days of observing them and assembled his "Comanches" to make sure they all understood their respective tasks. One by one, he questioned each man, and was satisfied that they were ready. Then Wilson raised his hand.

"What is it, Wilson?"

"Sergeant, I have some what-ifs that are bothering me. Like what if the pickets I'm supposed to get ain't where they're supposed to be? And what if a picket just happens to see us before we can get him? And what if I can't bring myself to slit his throat or stab him? It ain't like we was taking on Comanches.'"

A murmur of assent arose from the group, and a disturbed Sergeant England began pacing back and forth, wrestling with how to deal with this last-minute problem that could upset all the plans of Lee and his corps commanders.

Finally, he stopped, faced them, and began explaining why they had been called on for this mission. Then he said, "I'll give you another what-if to think about. What if I went to General Longstreet and told him that Texans were a bunch of cowards who could not be counted on to do their duty, and he would have to find some other troops who had the guts to do what the Texans could not."

There was total silence while they absorbed England's remarks. Then "Rattlesnake" Scott, sitting next to Wilson, stood up, and without looking at Wilson, said, "Sarge, count me in. I'll do what we have to do."

One by one, the others stood up until only Wilson remained seated. England looked at him, eyebrows raised questioningly.

"I'm sorry, Sarge, I just can't kill another American that way. And you know I ain't no coward!"

Scott spoke up. "That's true, Sarge, Will ain't no coward and we all know that."

"Alright, Wilson, you're excused. Scott, you and Robbins will take out the pickets that Wilson was assigned, in addition to the ones you already have. As for the other points Wilson raised, if you are discovered, we abort and get the hell back to General Longstreet. And if you can't find your pickets, let me know and we'll take it from there. We meet here tonight at midnight. Dismissed."

A now concerned England decided he should inform General Longstreet and see what came of that.

* * *

"General, I have just met with Sergeant England, the leader of the Comanche squad, who informed me that his people are having doubts about the ethics, I guess that's the right word, of what they have been asked to do. I . . ." Longstreet stopped when he saw Lee smile and raise his hand.

"Pete, I have also had those doubts and have just told Walter to inform you to modify the role of the Texans." Lee then explained what he wanted the Texans to do. He also told Longstreet of the cancellation of the prisoner release and the procedure for Pickett to follow.

Both the Comanche strike and the prisoner release had been Longstreet's ideas, and he found it difficult to hide the feeling that he had failed in his effort to take some of the weight off Lee in this difficult moment, but he managed to merely nod in agreement, and turned to leave.

"Pete, we will have a meeting here at noon to make sure that Hill and Ewell understand clearly what you and I have just discussed."

Longstreet recognized Lee's attempt to assuage any hurt feelings, and once again was filled with admiration for his commander-in-chief. This time, his smile was spontaneous as he saluted and left.

* * *

As Halleck had surmised, Meade was indeed unhappy about the delay of Ord's corps, and had displayed his infamous temper, but now he had calmed down and was deciding what to instruct Ord to do when more messages arrived, one from Grant and one from Ord, with Grant leaving matters in Ord's hands, and Ord informing Grant, Halleck and Meade that he intended to push on to Baltimore, there to board trains that he hoped would be waiting, and arrive at Martinsburg by noon of the ninth. Ord further stated that Thirteenth Corps, though somewhat worn, was ready for combat.

Meade was reassured by Ord's outlook and sent his concurrence in Ord's intentions. He additionally requested that Ord send location reports every four hours, beginning at 2 pm.

Unknowingly, Meade had taken a step that would play a crucial role in events to come.

MARYLAND

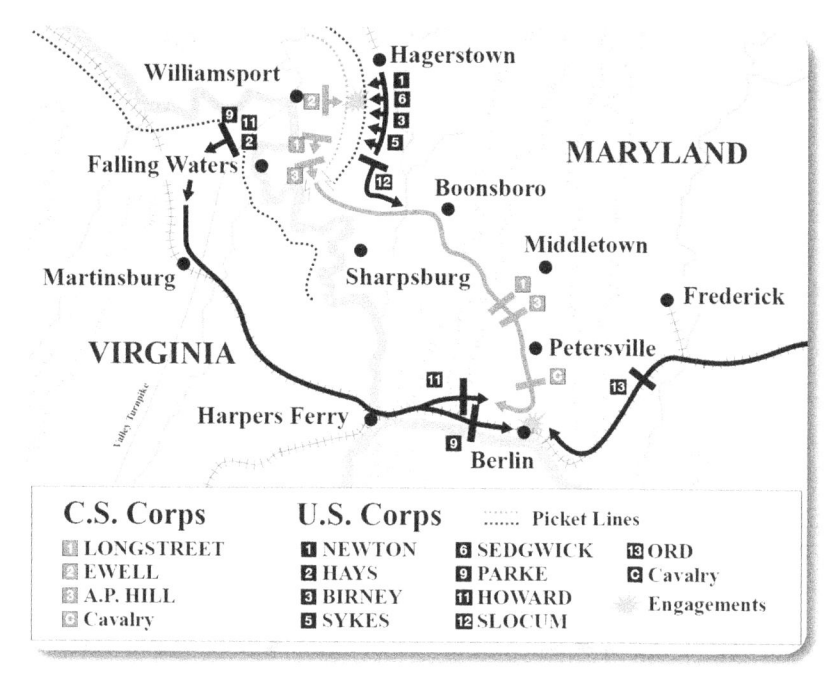

VIRGINIA

C.S. Corps
- 1 LONGSTREET
- 2 EWELL
- 3 A.P. HILL
- C Cavalry

U.S. Corps
- 1 NEWTON
- 2 HAYS
- 3 BIRNEY
- 5 SYKES
- 6 SEDGWICK
- 9 PARKE
- 11 HOWARD
- 12 SLOCUM
- 13 ORD
- C Cavalry

······· Picket Lines
✻ Engagements

Lee breaks siege.
©David John Murphy

JULY 9, 1863

It was midnight, and the rain had once again started to fall, lightly at first, then increasing in volume until now it was a steady, heavy downpour. The river had receded somewhat earlier during the day but was beginning to rise again. Lee had mixed feelings about the rain, which would aid in shielding their massing of the troops for the breakthrough but would also reduce their options to taking Baltimore or finding an intact bridge or ferry, provided, of course, that they were successful in breaking through the Union line.

The troops had enjoyed a full meal of beef and lamb, with the last of the potatoes and corn. The guards had shared the meal with their prisoners, and when asked what the occasion was, had mumbled something about a birthday. The sergeant of the guard said, "Yank, if I was you, I'd just be thankful to be getting this food, and leave it at that." That ended any further questions, with the Union prisoners eagerly downing their meals.

Longstreet was quietly conferring with Sergeant England. "Sergeant, take your squad and get into the very end of the Union line. Take down the first Yanks you see and keep doing so until we are discovered or until I tell you to stop, or until you see our troops moving through the opening you have made. Use your men to best effect thereafter."

England disappeared in the rain and darkness. Longstreet shivered but not from being cold on this warm and humid July night. It was an involuntary muscle reaction to the intense stress he was feeling; once he knew that England and his squad had cleared the way, the tension would ease, but until then, the shivers would continue. He remained in a secluded area to avoid being seen.

England joined his waiting men who were almost invisible, their faces, necks, ears, and even the back of their hands, were blackened with a mixture of coal oil and ashes.

England in a quiet voice said, "Let's go."

Their moccasined feet made no noise as they swiftly glided through the opening in the breastworks and headed for the extreme left end of the Union breastworks, where they stopped one by one until all were there. Then the first two silently crept over the Union breastworks, slithering in the wet dirt until inside. Crouching low, they listened for the sound of the pickets talking to one another. At first, the noise of the wind and rain masked all other sounds, but then a loud chuckle could be heard, and looking at each other, the two nodded and moved toward the sound, keeping bent low and close to the wall of the breastworks.

The pickets had no lights nor any fires due to the rain, but both were smoking pipes, and now their assailants could smell whiffs of burning tobacco and could see the faint glow of their pipes. Rushing simultaneously, the two Texans had their targets in neck holds that quickly rendered them unconscious. Laying the two pickets on the ground, they securely bound their hands and legs, and then gagged them. Two minutes had elapsed from start to finish.

In the meantime, as soon as the first two pickets were taken down, the other Texans silently ran by and in tandem, took down the Union pickets, during which the only sounds were those of the wind, rain, and an occasional picket chatting with his mate.

Twenty minutes later, England and his squad had cleared over a quarter mile of the Union line, and with instructions to his squad to be alert for any intruders into the cleared section of the Union line, England took off to report to Longstreet.

Longstreet had never felt such tension as he was feeling now. As the minutes passed and all remained quiet over at the Union side, he told himself that no noise was a good sign that England and his men were alright, but a nagging voice within argued that they could have been captured and even now were being interrogated.

His musings were abruptly interrupted when his arm was touched by Sergeant England who had appeared out of the pitch-black dark. A flood of relief filled Longstreet when England said the task was done and the Union side was soundly asleep.

Longstreet quickly mounted his horse, tossed a handful of cigars to England, and cantered off to find Lee.

Lee had been impatiently waiting for news from Longstreet, and when he saw him riding out of the darkness, he called out to Longstreet, asking if Longstreet was ready.

"Yes, sir, we await your order to move out."

"Make it so, General, and may God be kind to us and our cause."

Saluting, Longstreet swung his steed around and headed for the lead division. Normally it was McLaw's but tonight, Longstreet had placed Hood's division in the lead. Longstreet had done so based on intuition, but he had told McLaw it was to keep England's squad in touch with their Texas brethren, a reason a skeptical McLaw passed on to his troops, most of whom were readily willing to let the Texans lead the way.

Although wounded on the second day at Gettysburg, Hood had insisted on leading his division and was strapped into his saddle, awaiting the order to start occupying the Union line. That order now came from Longstreet, and the tension that always accompanied the wait to go into battle was broken as the troops moved into the break in their line of entrenchment and out into the area between the lines. Bending low, and moving swiftly but quietly, bayonets fixed, the lead troopers reached the Union breastwork and planted make-shift wooden ladders against the breastwork outer wall. Troops scrambled up, over, and into the Union line where they found the Union soldiers who had been bound and gagged by England's squad. It was Lee who had directed the Texans to kill only if they had no other choice.

As rehearsed during the past day, they now cautiously continued down the entrenchment, Colonel Law leading, continuing to find more Yanks who had been handled by England.

Law estimated that at least a quarter of a mile of the extreme left of the Union line had been breached when he encountered England and his men returning. England reported that they had cleared the next hundred yards or so and advised Law that the Yanks were positioned about every fifty yards, and if there had been no rain, he thought they would have been quickly noticed.

Law set up a human barrier of twenty men just shy of the next Yankee, and still undetected, began directing the remainder of his brigade to form a line of battle at right angle to the Union line. Hood came up, quickly surveyed the situation, and continued the formation of the rest of his division in line of battle.

In the area between the lines, Longstreet and McLaw's Division anxiously waited for word from Hood. Appearing out of the night it was Sergeant England who gave Longstreet the news that the Union line had been breached, having been detailed by Hood to carry the news.

Longstreet sent England on to Lee who was with Hill whose corps was originally to be in the center of the army's column. Lee realized that having Hood guarding the flank until Ewell could replace him would delay Longstreet, so he had just now ordered Hill to move out and take the lead.

The Union bombardment had ceased while the gun crews changed, but suddenly the bursting of a shell erupted a shower of mud that caused no casualties, but did increase the urgency for the need to get moving,

* * *

It was now almost three o'clock and so far, everything was proceeding according to the plan. Hill's corps had cleared the Union line, followed by Longstreet, and then the rain began to stop. Ewell's corps, which had been manning the Confederate line, was falling into formation when a sheet of lightning creased the sky, illuminating the Confederates. Almost immediately, three shots were heard, the signal for the Union army that trouble was afoot. Bugles began sounding the call to arms, and shouts of sergeants could be heard, getting troops ready.

Ewell immediately ordered his corps to return to the breastworks but almost fifteen minutes were lost in countermanding his previous orders and getting the men over the muddy, slippery dirt walls of their breastworks. Unlike the other corps, Second Corps had issued twenty rounds to each man since they had to man the line while First and Third Corps evacuated. Rifled muskets loaded, they stood in battle formation, awaiting the expected attack by the Yanks.

Ewell had lost part of his artillery to the Yankee mortars, as well as a number of artillerymen, but Lieutenant Colonel Porter Alexander, Longstreet's chief of artillery, had voluntarily stayed behind to cover the loss of Ewell's chief of artillery, killed by one of the Union mortar rounds. He now directed the placement of the corps' remaining six batteries, drawing some of the mortar firing away from the breastworks.

Both Lee and Longstreet had heard the shots fired by the Union picket, but Hill had not, and he continued to push his corps of 13,000 or so along the river-side road, heading for the junction with the National Pike, the route to Baltimore. Hill's last order from General Lee had been to occupy Baltimore as quickly as possible, and to begin commandeering all ships in the harbor that were large enough to carry troops and their equipment. Hill's men were in high spirits as they marched headlong into the night.

Upon hearing the three shots, Longstreet ordered his corps to halt. It took several minutes for the order to reach the regiments, with some stopping while others barged into those stopped, causing growing confusion, abetted by the pitch-black night. The regiments in the rear had not received the order to halt, and the lead ranks were pushing into the stopped troops, cursing at them to get moving, while those who had halted cursed back, informing the regiments trying to march through of the order to halt. What had been a smoothly executed plan was rapidly deteriorating into blundering chaos. It would be another ten minutes before order was restored.

In the meantime, Lee was seeking Longstreet, while also trying to get the men back into ranks. The black night that had aided their escape was now proving to be a severe hindrance. A large flash of lightning lasted several seconds, enabling Walter Taylor to see Longstreet and bring him to Lee.

Both assumed that Hill had heard the three shots, and Lee was issuing orders to his staff to inform Hill to come up on Longstreet's right and to dig in on a line running northeast from Longstreet, with his right-most three regiments refused, unless there was a good terrain feature upon which to anchor his flank.

Longstreet was getting his corps massed in what he expected would be the middle, once Ewell arrived, but so far nothing had been heard from Ewell. He concluded that Ewell's corps had been discovered preparing to leave. Longstreet approached Lee. "Sir, it seems that Ewell might be trapped since there is no sign of his corps."

Lee turned to Longstreet, paused, then said, "If that is so, Ewell has been instructed to stay and resist as long as possible so as to hold the enemy while we open the distance sufficiently to allow us to gain Baltimore. If you are satisfied that Ewell was not able to clear the lines, we must resume the march quickly."

The matter-of-fact manner in the way Lee informed Longstreet of the sacrifice of Ewell and his corps was upsetting to Longstreet, and while he recognized the logic, he found it difficult to accept.

Wheeling his horse, Longstreet galloped back to the road where there still was no sign of Ewell. He then rode up and down the line of troops, giving orders to get them back on the road and moving out. It was then that he saw that Hill had continued to move, and he wondered if Hill had known of Lee's orders to Ewell. The specter of Jackson was ever present, and now it loomed larger because he knew that Jackson would have no troubles with Lee"s decision. *Get your mind on your duty, and make sure that Ewell's sacrifice is not in vain.*

* * *

The black night was an impartial actor, affecting Meade just as it affected Lee. Meade had sent several of his staff to do a rapid reconnaissance to determine what the Confederates were up to and was impatiently awaiting their return when he heard a voice behind him. It had been over half an hour since the alarm had sounded.

"General Meade!"

Meade turned. "Yes, who calls?"

"Sir, I am Lieutenant Wilson, the duty siege battery officer." Meade saw a young Marine officer carrying a lantern. Wilson continued, "Request permission to fire star shells over the Rebel lines to illuminate them for our gunners to identify targets."

"Yes, do so, and bring all your batteries on line. It looks like this may be the attempt by Lee to break the siege."

"Aye, aye, sir!" A crisp salute and the Marine was gone.

In a little more than five minutes, the siege guns began hurling star shells, one every fifteen seconds, lighting up the night, revealing Confederate troops hastily moving into the center of the Rebel breastworks. They could be seen fortifying their flanks. So, whose men were these? Who had already marched out when the discovery of the breakout occurred? And where were they?

An agitated Slocum appeared. It was his sector where the Confederates escaped. When the rifle shots were heard, the ensuing noise awakened Slocum, who was hurriedly slipping on his uniform when Alpheus Williams stuck his head through the tent flap with the news of finding their pickets bound and gagged. He then informed Slocum that Hill and Longstreet had taken their corps out and were moving down the river road. Ewell's corps had been on the verge of getting out as well but had turned back when the alarm had sounded. It was Ewell's men who now manned the center sector of the Confederate lines.

* * *

After Slocum informed Meade of all this, Meade now had a fair picture of where Hill and Longstreet were heading. Calling for his communications sergeant, he dictated a message to Grant, Halleck, and Ord, requesting that Ord and his corps move into position to block Lee's two corps that likely would be heading east on the National Road in order to occupy Baltimore. He added that the details surrounding their escape would follow, but it was urgent that Ord start now to set up a strong blocking position. Meade closed by saying that Ewell had not been able to follow Hill and Longstreet and would be contained within the Confederate lines for the time being.

The heavy siege mortars were delivering a steady barrage of star shells and exploding rounds that were causing a mounting number of casualties among Ewell's corps, especially those manning the breastworks, and one by one these men began seeking shelter in the bombproofs they had previously erected during the siege. Ewell was himself slightly wounded by a shell fragment and was being treated for the wound to his arm when he noted more casualties arriving. One of them, a tall older soldier, spoke to him.

"Gen'ral, you know we Virginians have never run from them Yanks in a battle, but it don't make sense to stand out there and just die without doing a damned thing to them Yanks." A chorus of voices agreed.

"Gen'ral, meanin' no disrespect, but I think we should either go out there and fight, or we should raise the white flag."

Shouts of "Fight!" were mixed with other shouts of "White flag!" It was hearing the latter, the first time Ewell had ever heard his Virginians call for such, that made him consider such a course. He would not surrender, but he realized the futility of continuing to man the breastworks, and he ordered his troops to seek shelter until the shelling stopped. By this time, the rain had stopped, and the clearing sky was showing the glimmering streaks of dawn.

With his field glasses, Lieutenant Wilson was closely observing the effect of the shelling and he now shouted, "They're leaving the breastworks!" Ordering the battery to continue their deadly work, Wilson ran the several hundred yards to Meade's headquarters where he burst in on Meade and Slocum.

"Sir! The Rebs are being forced off their works by our shelling!"

Meade grabbed his field glasses and stepped outside, followed by Slocum. The eastern sky was brightening with the rising sun, the rain having stopped and the clouds breaking. Meade lowered his field glasses and turned to Wilson.

"Continue your fire until you see our troops advancing. You and your gunners have done well, Lieutenant."

"Aye, sir, thank you, sir" A quick salute, and Wilson was gone.

Meade turned to Slocum. "General, prepare your corps to pursue Longstreet and Hill. You will be joined by Newton, Hays and Birney. Sedgwick and Sykes will handle Ewell. Parke and Howard will proceed by train to Baltimore to join Ord, who is taking a blocking position on the National Road west of Baltimore. March lightly, bullets and beans will be following closely."

Humphreys had assembled the staff and now began dispatching couriers to the corps commanders with verbal orders, to be followed by detailed orders in writing.

As Slocum was mounting his horse, he exchanged a quick glance with Humphreys, a look that said their commanding general was showing that he no longer needed anyone's counsel; he had things well in hand.

* * *

Contrary to Ewell's order for the men to take shelter, Jubal Early was ordering his division, now numbering less than 4,000 men, to return to their section of the breastworks, cursing and raging as only Early could. Defying the shells exploding and the shards of hot metal bursting around him, Early stood up on top of the breastworks, waving his sword and yelling his defiance of the blankety-blank blue-bellies and his scorn for any cowards among his division who could not face their foes like men.

He remained somehow unscathed, and his men sheepishly sidled back to their posts on the line, but the intensity of the shelling increased, and the casualties began increasing. Then, the shelling stopped, and the ensuing silence left the troops with ears hearing echoes from the blasting.

It was daylight now, and peering through the gun hole in the breastworks, a sergeant saw a sight that sent his heart racing in the expectation of battle. "Here they come, boys," he shouted. Heads poked above the works and what they saw brought gasps of awe.

Silently advancing across the mile-wide space between the Union and Confederates lines were the combined corps of Sykes and Sedgwick, ranks aligned, flags fluttering, bayonets gleaming in the brightening sunlight, but silently, no drums beating, no orders being shouted. On they came, steadily and unwavering, no cheering, just silence.

Once again, Jubal Early mounted the works, waving his sword and shouting. Without stopping, several dozen in the front rank of the advancing Federals raised their loaded rifles and fired. Early half-turned, dropped his sword, and slumped to the ground, a look of disbelief on his face. Early was dead, a bullet in his heart.

Elsewhere along the works, troops were running to their posts and began firing at the advancing troops in blue, some of whom fell but the ranks quickly closed and on they came. At the same time, Alexander got his batteries manned and they also commenced firing, their canister ripping large holes in the blue ranks.

 Suddenly, they broke the silence with a loud cheer, breaking into a run, bayonets lowered. Hundreds of Confederates fired into the blue ranks, now less than a hundred yards away and closing swiftly. The Rebel artillery could no longer fire without hitting their own men. Hundreds of the infantry still fired, ripping unfilled holes in the front ranks, slowing and then halting the advance. But now the Confederates began to run out of ammunition, and their firing dropped off.

Sensing the change, the Fifth and Sixth Corps re-formed their ranks, and charged again. This time, they were met with bayonets and knives as they scaled the Rebel works. Desperate men engaged in brutal and fierce combat, a highly personal, face to face, stabbing and slashing kind of combat.

Melee at Harper's Ferry
iStock.com

Ewell's men fought valiantly, but so did the Yanks. Out-flanked and out-numbered, pockets of surrendering Confederates began to appear. Ewell, his men out of bullets and powder, raised the white flag. For the Second Corps of the Army of Northern Virginia, the war was over.

As if Nature was sympathizing with the Rebels, thick gray clouds, blown by a north-easterly wind, came scudding across the sky, painting the fields a somber hue. Fifth Corps had been assigned the task of getting the Confederate prisoners to the temporary stockade that had been hastily erected for holding them while waiting for the trains that would take them to other trains hauling boxcars modified for the single purpose of transporting prisoners of war

* * *

After a brief meeting with Sykes and Sedgwick, Ewell had been taken to a nearby field hospital where he was getting his wounded arm cleaned and bandaged under the watchful eye of Dr. Letterman, senior medical officer of the Union army. It was there that he was joined by Major General Johnson, commander of one of Ewell's divisions.

"I find it difficult to accept the role of sacrificial offering," Johnson muttered. "How could General Lee do this, and not even speak to us about it!?"

Looking up, Ewell quietly said, "He spoke to me yesterday. Asked me if I would be willing to stay and fight long enough to keep Meade occupied in the event that the breakout was discovered before we were out. We almost made it, but when I heard the rifle shots, I knew we had a choice; we could either turn and fight or we could try to get out. It was my call. The continued existence of the Army of Northern Virginia is an absolute requirement that comes before any single corps, because the fate of the Confederacy will be determined by what happens to our army."

Both men were silent for a moment. Then Johnson said, with head bowed, "Thank you, sir. I just wish we had known this before. It would have made our men fight much harder and longer if they had known."

Ewell nodded in agreement. "Unfortunately, there was not enough time to inform the men or even you, but we must somehow communicate this to them now, if possible. If you can speak quietly to the officers, perhaps some of them could slip in among the troops and explain why we did what we did."

And that's how Ewell's men learned why their fellow Confederates called them heroes.

* * *

Haupt managed to get trains for Ord, and the Thirteenth Corps had arrived in Baltimore as dawn was lighting the horizon in the east. Halleck and Grant were both at Camden Station and greeted Ord with the news that Lee had slipped out and appeared to be heading for Baltimore. Both boarded Ord's car and Halleck broke out a map of the area. Grant pointed to the western boundary of Baltimore, then moved his finger to the Patapsco River, just west of the boundary.

"The Patapsco crosses the National Pike through a deep ravine that extends several miles north and south of the road. General Halleck and

I made a quick tour of the area and it has what appears to be some good terrain for defense. There is a road seven miles north of here that could be used for a flanking movement, so you will want to keep an eye on it.

"John Buford has a small brigade in his division that is being used to track Lee, commanded by Wesley Merritt. The last report from Merritt placed the head of Hill's corps near New Market. Hill has the lead, with Longstreet following. Meade is several miles behind Lee. I have assumed overall command and have asked Meade to be ready to oppose a reverse march by Lee, and not to close any nearer than he is now.

"There is a bridge at that road to the north that should be destroyed if the Rebels try to flank or bypass you. New Market is a good eight hours away, and with them marching all night, it may be ten hours before their van arrives here. We know that Lee has only enough ammo for one day of combat, and Ewell's corps no longer exists, so I think we have the advantage. Let's make the most of it."

Halleck failed to notice that Grant had overlooked the Ninth and Eleventh Corps and did not include them.

Grant and Halleck departed, Ord issued orders for the corps to move out, and then he and his corps engineer mounted to do a quick check of the Patapsco.

* * *

Stuart had watched the fate of the Second Corps unfold and now it was with heavy heart that he described to Lee the loss of Ewell and his command. Longstreet was nearby and heard it all. He knew that General Lee deeply felt the anguish caused by the loss of one of his corps. He saw Lee's head bow, lips compressed, eyes shut. Then once more, Lee was his usual dignified, erect, self-contained person, commanding the respect of friend and foe.

"General Stuart, I need to know if those people who were blocking us at Williamsport are still there or, if not, where they are. And where is Ord? What is the location of Meade? Are Sykes and Sedgwick still up by Williamsport?"

As Stuart turned his mount and departed, Lee turned to Walter Taylor. "Do you have Jed's map of this area?"

Taylor reached into his saddle bag and extracted the cylinder of heavy paper used by Hotchkiss for the map. Unrolling it, Taylor held it for Lee, who studied it intensely for a moment. Then, "Walter, be alert for the junction of the road to Harper's Ferry. If we could cross there, we would be once again on Virginian soil and a day's march from Winchester, whereas if we go to Baltimore, we will have to find and commandeer enough craft to transport us all in one intact group. I suspect we will find Meade's Ninth and Eleventh Corps either already at Harpers Ferry or on the way."

The head of Longstreet's column was approaching the point where the road to Harpers Ferry nosed perpendicularly into the National Pike, when the scout sent to Harpers Ferry appeared in the distance.

Longstreet halted the escort cavalry riding ahead of the column and waited for the scout's report. He was joined by Taylor.

Saluting, the scout, a lean, sunburned man about the same age as Longstreet, reported, "General, there are two corps of Yanks approaching the railroad bridge at Harpers Ferry. One corps I identified as the Eleventh, but I saw no regimental colors for the other fellows. I understand from hearing some of their pickets talking that the other corps is from Ohio, most likely the Yankee Ninth."

One by one, the other scouts began arriving, each making his report immediately upon arrival. Meade was a good eight miles west of the rear ranks of the column. The scout reported seeing four corps with Meade.

The last scout to come in arrived a few minutes later, and riding up to Lee, stayed mounted, saluting aa he reined in. "General, I never found Ord but I talked to some people in a village about twenty miles from here who told me that his corps had passed through there late yesterday. Said they looked a lot like us 'stead of the Yanks we been fighting."

"Did those villagers say in what direction they were marching?"

"Yes, sir, said they were heading for Baltimore."

Lee was silent as he studied the map. Meade was behind him, two corps were at Harpers Ferry, and Ord was somewhere to the east, between them and Baltimore. Federals to the northwest, to the southwest, and somewhere to the east. Lee had turned south at Boonsboro and was now at Petersville, a move that Stuart's cavalry screen had concealed from the Union cavalry scouts led by Merritt. Lee saw a choice of moves he could make. He could lay a trap for the corps crossing at Harpers Ferry; he could continue on to

Baltimore and take on Ord when and if encountered; or he could head to Berlin some ten miles south and cross on the large bridge he knew was there. Both of the first two possible moves entailed the prospect of battle, which meant using his limited supply of ammunition, and incurred delay in reaching Virginia. He could probably replenish his ammunition in Baltimore, provided that he was able to sweep Ord aside with the rounds on hand. The same problem existed in taking on the two corps at Harpers Ferry, with the additional risk of being overtaken by Meade before completing the defeat of Parke and Howard.

That left Berlin, ten miles to the south. Or did it?

Lee had entered Pennsylvania with three objectives, two of which had been attained, namely, food for his army and respite for the people of Virginia. The third objective, the neutralizing of the Army of the Potomac, he had failed to meet. Another look at the map showed the Union forces sufficiently far from one another so as to offer an opportunity to defeat them in detail, a tempting prospect that, if successful, could have far-reaching consequences. If Meade were to be badly whipped after holding off Lee at Gettysburg, the morale of the North might suffer to the point of causing Lincoln to sue for peace, and for Britain and France to recognize the Confederate States as a legitimate nation.

In considering adopting the idea, the scarcity of ammunition and artillery rounds was certainly a disadvantage, but only if he failed to overcome his adversary in the first encounter, therefore choosing which force to fight first would be a critical decision.

Merritt was attempting to penetrate Stuart's screen by use of scattered patrols. He had stopped at a local farm for a quick breakfast when one of the patrols came in with two of Stuart's troopers. When questioned, neither would say anything. Merritt said to tie them to a nearby hitching post, and as they were being taken away, he told the sergeant to let the younger one escape. He was to be followed, thereby leading them to Lee's location.

Within the hour, Merritt knew that Lee was at the junction of the National Pike and the Harpers Ferry Road.

* * *

Any officer with combat experience knows that plans and orders are one thing while the execution thereof is usually quite another. Plans can be made and orders issued based upon the best information at hand as well as the best estimate of the enemy's intent. But information might be inaccurate, and the enemy's intent might be misunderstood; both often were. The military term for this is "the fog of war."

And then there is the every-day kind of mishap, such as Ord failing to receive the copy addressed to him of the message to Parke and Howard, informing them of Lee's location, directing them to destroy the bridge at Berlin, and then to proceed to join Ord at Baltimore. If Ord had known that two corps would be joining him, he might have planned differently.

* * *

Grant had been following the progress of events as reported by Meade, as well as Sedgwick and Ord. The last report by Merritt of Lee's location placed him at Boonesboro. That had been over six hours ago, and Merritt had just reported that he had lost contact due to heavy Confederate cavalry interference. Meade was assuming that Lee was heading for Baltimore, but, Grant wondered, if that was his objective, why had he not been sighted at Frederick by now?

Grant noted that, at Boonesboro, two roads intersected the National Pike, a road running southwest to Harpers Ferry and a road running south to Berlin. He also noted that both places had bridges crossing into Virginia. If he were Lee, where would he go, now that he apparently had turned off the National Pike? Parke and Howard were at Harpers Ferry, but Berlin was uncovered.

Parke and Howard, at Harpers Ferry, were only five miles from Berlin, and Meade was knocking at Lee's back door.

Grant turned to Halleck, told him to send messages to Meade, Parke and Ord, advising them that indications were that Lee was somewhere between Boonesboro and Berlin, followed by Grant ordering Parke and Howard to destroy the bridge at Berlin, and to hold at the Maryland side of the railroad bridge at Harpers Ferry. With Meade closing on his rear, Lee would not have time to try to overcome Parke and Howard. With the Berlin bridge destroyed, Lee would be left with Baltimore as his only option.

When queried, Meade reported his location at Middletown, sixteen miles from Berlin. What Meade did not know was that Lee at this moment was just seven miles away at Petersville, watching as the first brigade of Hill's corps was marching out of the town. A mile ahead, Longstreet's corps was disappearing around a sharp curve in the road.

The sun was breaking through the clouds, and a cool breeze out of the north was holding the temperature in the high seventies. Barn swallows swooped above the heads of the troops, gathering the insects disturbed by the marchers. Other birds, high in the trees, chirped and sang their unique songs. Lee's men took the break in the weather as a good sign, and they set out with renewed vigor.

* * *

The trooper who had "escaped" was telling Stuart of his encounter with Merritt. Stuart commended him for making his escape. The trooper then informed Stuart that he and his sergeant had scouted east as far as Mount Airy and had found no sign of Ord or of any Federals between them and Baltimore. "That means the road to Baltimore is open."

Lee was silent as he considered his choices now. He was so close to crossing into Virginia, but the prospect of whipping Meade was so tempting. If he dallied too long, the Yankees would start closing in, which meant he would probably have to engage their united forces in combat with limited ammunition for his men and for his artillery. Baltimore could supply both, as well as boats to transport his army to Virginia. Could the troops, who had been marching for almost ten hours now, continue on to Baltimore, about thirty miles distant, without stopping? Jackson had done a similar march from the Blue Ridge to Manassas Junction in 1862, but Jackson now was in the cemetery at Lexington. Shaking his head, Lee said, "Desperate situations justify desperate measures. The way to Baltimore is open and once there, we can re-supply our ammunition. It will depend upon the ability of our men to march another thirty miles." Lee raised a questioning look at Longstreet and Hill. In the back of Lee's mind was the possibility of ambushing Meade if the terrain somewhere between Frederick and Baltimore offered such.

Longstreet hesitated, but Hill was shaking his head.

"Meade is only an hour behind us, with troops in much better condition than ours. We'll never make it to Baltimore. If we move rapidly over the short distance to Berlin, we can handle Howard and that other corps before Meade catches up, and use the bridge at Berlin."

Lee turned toward the river, and while considering Hill's argument, an explosion, followed by three more, echoed and re-echoed from the direction of Berlin.

"Those people seem to have decided our course for us," Lee said in a grim tone. "Continue the march to Baltimore."

Stuart spoke. "Sir, let me try to secure the bridge at Harpers Ferry. If I can get there before Howard, we might be able to cross before Meade can stop us."

Lee nodded, and Stuart hurried off. It was worth the try, but in the meantime, Lee ordered Hill to move out; he could double back if Stuart was successful.

* * *

Merritt's scout had observed the trooper's brief meeting with Stuart, and had followed Stuart at a discreet distance, his effort rewarded by sight of Lee himself. Noting the location, he cautiously cleared the area and then spurred his mount to a full gallop, but not back to Merritt. Instead, he rode into Berlin, arriving as Parke's leading division was entering from the west. The scout, whose name was Radford, West Point 1852, had seen Parke's corps as it approached Berlin, and decided that he should warn Parke that Lee was just an hour or so away, and Stuart might appear in force at any time. He then left to report to Merritt.

Parke called for his pioneers and asked them to do a quick survey of the bridge to see if they could destroy it with explosives.

The senior pioneer returned with the news that they could place explosives at the ends of each span and drop the spans. The abutments were another matter, being built of large chiseled stones and mortar. Planks could be laid to replace the dropped spans but would have to be about forty feet long. With Parke's approval, the pioneers began placing explosives at the ends of each span where it joined the abutment. At the same time, the two corps began working on setting up breastworks with trees and dirt.

A half hour later, the charges exploded, sending large clouds of dust and debris in the air, and dropping the spans in the river. The noise made by the explosions reverberated between the low elevations on each side of the river, causing large flocks of geese and ducks to take flight. At that moment, the van of the Army of Northern Virginia appeared, coming over the rise some three miles from Berlin.

Raising his field glasses, Parke saw them halt. An excited buzz arose from his boys in blue as they craned to see their opponents in gray and butternut, the vaunted Southrons led by Robert E. Lee. Soon, five officers on mounts appeared, and Parke watched as they all scanned the bridge that no longer could be crossed. He easily identified Lee, and then Longstreet and Hill. Then the long plume in the hat of the fourth officer helped to identify Stuart. Lee said something to Stuart, who looked in the direction of Harpers Ferry, and dashed off. Lee and the others turned and disappeared behind the rise, followed by the troops in the van. A minute later, there were no Rebs to be seen.

Stuart had looked in the direction of Harpers Ferry. Parke quickly mounted and galloped to where Howard was overseeing the placing of his artillery.

Parke shouted as he rode up, "Harpers Ferry! Lee is going to head for Harpers Ferry. Extend your line westward sufficient to block the Harpers Ferry Road. I will move my troops to the right of you."

Howard began shifting his brigades and as they took up positions across the Harpers Ferry Road, two columns of Confederate cavalry came cantering over the rise where Lee had appeared. There was a low stone wall running across the open field that lay between the Blue and the Gray, extending more than a half mile. The two brigades in the field took cover behind the wall and began firing at the Confederates, who were swinging into a double line of battle, the maneuver executed with precision. Then, with sabers leveled, the Confederated broke into full gallop as they charged across the wide pasture.

"Fix bayonets!" was ordered and the stone wall now was a wall of bayonets, held with the rifle butts pressed against the ground. Behind those manning the bayonets other troops were steadily loading and firing at the oncoming Confederates, who began taking casualties. Howard's artillery opened now with blasts of canister, adding to the toll of Confederate casualties.

But on they came, hooves pounding louder and louder as they thundered toward the Yankee line. The sight of the horses mounted by mad men holding long sabers pointed at them caused some men to break and run. Others holding bayonets thrust them upward as the Confederates charged over the wall, stabbing into the horses and riders, and losing their weapons that were ripped out of their hands. A chaotic melee of men and horses, many now without riders, saw pistols fired at point-blank range, rifles became murderous clubs, and sabers were slashing and drawing blood.

Out-numbered by the Yankee infantry, the hard-pressed Rebels fell back and cantered their exhausted mounts back across the field and over the rise.

No sooner had they gone when another type of foe began to appear, with regimental flags fluttering and drums beating, it was the entire Third Corps of the Army of Northern Virginia moving in battle formation. But it was not the usual battle formation.

The center of the formation was occupied by a solid column of infantry that a quick count showed to be fifty men wide and an estimated one hundred fifty men deep. On each side, at irregular spacing and moving erratically was a swarm of about two thousand troops, resembling a swarm of bees or hornets.

Seeing the Rebel infantry coming *en masse*, Parke re-assessed the situation. In less than a minute, he ordered Ninth Corps to dig in behind Eleventh Corps and between Eleventh and the Harpers Ferry bridge. This would provide defense in depth and enable a retro-movement toward the bridge, making the Confederates fight every step of the way to reach the bridge.

The planks that had been laid over the railroad tracks on the bridge had been removed and were stowed in the Engine House, the sturdy brick building where John Brown had been captured by Marines commanded by Colonel R. E. Lee, US Army, assisted by a young dragoon officer named Stuart.

* * *

Grant stepped off the train as soon as it stopped at Frederick where he was met by Major General William French, commanding the 5,000-man garrison protecting Frederick. Wasting troops on garrison duty was a constant irritant for Grant, and his displeasure with the arrangement at Frederick showed in his gruff manner.

Without more than a brief nod of acknowledgement, Grant quickly mounted the horse French had provided, and briskly headed out to the road that would take him to Meade, followed by the squadron of cavalry that had been detailed by Meade to escort him. It was Grant who, after plotting the locations of the various units,, had seen the opportunity for Ord to play a decisive role at Harpers Ferry. Thirteenth Corps was already aboard a set of trains, waiting to proceed to Frederick, and it was a simple matter to move a few switches in the railroad yard and they pulled out headed for Harpers Ferry with throttles wide open, while Grant took a different train to Frederick.

The young captain leading the squadron, Charles Norris, moved up alongside Grant, after sending ten troopers ahead to give warning of any Rebels that might be in the vicinity.

Grant removed the cigar he was biting on and asked Norris about his outfit.

"Sir, I'm attached to General Buford's staff, and these troopers are Eighth Illinois, part of Buford's command." Anticipating Grant's next question, Norris added, "We should arrive at General Meade's headquarters in about twenty minutes, sir."

Grant glanced at Norris, who was visually checking on the outriders and appreciated Meade sending a savvy staffer rather than an officer whose knowledge would be limited to just his own outfit. Grant used the time to get a better and more timely picture of the situation. He was pleased to hear that Howard and Parke had repulsed Hill's first attack, but Norris had departed for Frederick with the outcome still not resolved. He told Grant that it appeared that Hill had taken heavy casualties but was still returning to the attack as he was departing. The lack of adequate supplies of bullets and powder, together with limited artillery support, had considerably hampered Hill's attack, despite the unique attack formation he had employed. Any further questions were forestalled by their arrival at Meade's temporary headquarters, a wagon guarded by a squad of infantry.

Grant thanked Captain Norris, dismounted, and returned Meade's salute. Taking Meade aside, Grant informed him that he had Lincoln's permission to grant Lee and his army liberal terms of surrender in return for their parole to lay down their arms permanently, never again to fight for the Confederacy. If Lee refused, Grant intended to make it clear that Lee would bear sole responsibility for the ensuing losses of men who otherwise could have returned to their families. Grant then listened carefully to Meade who quickly briefed him on the situation and the intended course of action.

Suddenly, the noise of battle rose dramatically. It was Ord's corps hammering Hill in a broad flanking attack.

* * *

When Stuart arrived to report the failed attempt to secure the bridge, he noted that Lee had Hill facing Parke and Howard, while Longstreet was in line of battle behind hastily erected breastworks evidently awaiting the appearance of Meade and the rest of the Army of the Potomac. He reasoned that Hill must have been joined by Longstreet in opposing marching to Baltimore, and with both of his corps commanders disagreeing with him, Lee had decided to try the Harpers Ferry route.

Lee acknowledged Stuart's report and appeared to have a question for Stuart when his attention abruptly shifted to the sudden sound of heavy cannonading and the sharp cracks of rifles fired in unison, coming from the direction of Hill's attack against the two Union corps barring the road to Harpers Ferry. Lee saw the leading ranks of the Confederate column blown away, causing a temporary halt. Then the column lunged forward, the high-pitched Rebel yell from thousands of voices competing with the continuous thunder of the Union artillery and the sharp crack of rifles. Bayonets gleaming in the bright sunlight, carried by men desperately trying to break through the defenders of the bridge, reflected the transformation of the Rebel column into a mob of wild-eyed men bent on relieving their anger and frustration by tearing through those devils in blue.

Grape, canister, and thousands of minie balls took down scores of the attackers, but scores more closed in and broke the line held by von Steinwehr's division, smothering Coster's brigade, and charging into the Second Brigade that stubbornly resisted, bending but not breaking.

The gap in the Union line created by the disintegration of von Steinwehr's First Brigade was being exploited by the Confederates whose rearward ranks now spread out, attacking Schurz's division on the Union right and Ames on the left.

The Confederates had mostly used up the sparse amounts of ammunition they had, and they began using the bayonet with considerable effect. The two divisions of Ames and Schurz had held on their fronts, but the pressure of the column of Confederates now began to force the Federals back. They were near the breaking point when the left flank of the Confederate column began to feel the sting of bullets that came seemingly out of nowhere, causing the Confederates to turn and face this new attack on their flank. Those who could see through the heavy smoke from burnt powder were shocked to see a line of battle comprised of men whose threadbare uniforms with blankets slung over the shoulder made them at first appear to the Confederates as also Confederates. But as they rapidly closed on the Confederate column, the faded blue of their uniforms became more visible. It was Ord's Thirteenth Corps, late of the Union Army of the Tennessee, now part of the Army of the Potomac, and eager to take on the Virginians.

Ord's 13th Corps strikes Confederate flank at Harper's Ferry.
iStock.com

The Confederate column was shattered by Ord's headlong attack on their flank. Hill's attack devolved into a stabbing, shooting, clubbing, hand-to-hand melee. Ames and Schurz took advantage of the ease in pressure to first stabilize their lines, quickly followed by a countercharge that drove the Rebels back into the melee caused by Ord's attack. Within minutes, Hill's corps was transformed into pockets with no escape, and those not yet surrounded hastened back to the Confederate lines.

Hill's corps had lost almost thirty per cent in dead and wounded, and now began to lose more as prisoners, despite the efforts of officers to extricate their units and return to where they could form again for another attack. More and more troops were seeing the futility of trying to break through the Union line; more and more began to surrender.

Seeing the disintegration of Hill's corps, and noting the exposure of Ord's right flank, Longstreet ordered his corps to about face as they stood in battle formation. With an assenting nod from Lee, Longstreet ordered the buglers to sound the charge. The veterans of Second Manassas recognized immediately what was intended, and with that keening Rebel yell, led the corps' leading division in a headlong charge that struck the flank of Ord's corps like a massive hammer, causing the Westerners to reel back, desperately fighting to stem the attack. Unlike the troops of Pope's army that had panicked and had run on that field of 1862, the men from Wisconsin, and Iowa, and Minnesota, and Indiana and Illinois, did not break and run, but their attack against Hill's corps was stopped dead.

Now Longstreet threw in his second division and was urging them to strike any group of blue in the mob of men fighting hand-to-hand with whatever could be found, including rocks, musket butts, bayonets, knives and even brass knuckles. Bloodied men continued to stand and fight until knocked down or stabbed so badly their legs gave way. It was then that Lee and Longstreet heard the piercing notes of a trumpet, louder than the bugle common to the armies. As the stirring notes of the Charge with their iambic rapid repetition continued, Lee and Longstreet saw the regimental flags of Slocum's Twelfth Corps come over the rise of the hill from which Longstreet had launched his attack. Still feeling the sting of having Lee make his escape from Williamsport through his sector, Slocum had force-marched his corps that arrived now well ahead of the rest of the corps that were with Meade.

The 13th New Jersey was in line of battle between the 2nd Massachusetts on their left and the 107th New York on their right. Ruger's Third Brigade anchored the right flank of the corps' battle line and Ruger had placed the 27th Indiana and the 3rd Wisconsin in the second rank behind the other three regiments. Moving at a trot, the troops fixed bayonets and on command, halted, loaded, and again on command, resumed the charge. Colonel Carman, with sword pointed ahead, was on foot in the van of his regiment. Now only a few hundred yards separated them from the rear ranks of Longstreet's corps, ranks that still had some semblance of order. The Yanks saw a tall, bearded officer suddenly appear, and as he shouted something, they saw those rear ranks turnabout and level their rifles with bayonets fixed, holding them alongside the right hip, creating a formidable wall of deadly steel.

Now some of the Rebels, not all, raised their rifles, aimed and fired, the reports of their guns slightly behind the smoke that erupted from their barrels. Bullets zipped past, making that sound of bees that veterans knew so well. Some of the bullets found their target, and men dropped here and there. Captain Bumsted saw Colonel Carman go down with a bullet in his left thigh. There being no time for determining seniority among the various company commanders, Bumsted, recognizing the need for a leader to keep the attack moving, immediately stepped out to the front of the formation. With a wave of the sword, he and the 13th broke into a run. With a ripple-like effect, the other regiments also began to run, a primal roar of battle lust rose from the ranks, venting months of frustration and the desire to overcome the foe. Just before reaching the Confederate ranks, the Union officers shouted the order to fire, and a devastating volley of bullets tore great holes in the Rebel formation.

As the Twelfth Corps slammed into Longstreet's people, the sound of bugles and now drums, coming from the hill behind Slocum's corps, added to the cacophony of battle. Looking toward the hill, Lee saw the rest of the Army of the Potomac descending in a giant envelopment of the struggling men in blue and grey mixed with butternut.

At that point, Lee realized that further combat was useless, nay, worse than useless in needlessly adding to the casualties on both sides. On Lee's order, his bugler sounded "cease fire," repeating it while other buglers on both sides took up the same call.

* * *

Quiet descended upon the field, and the men on both sides drifted back into loose formations. The only sounds now to be heard were the moans and cries for aid coming from the fallen.

Lee mounted Traveler with the intent to find Meade and offer his sword in surrender, an act he dreaded but felt honor-bound to carry out. As he turned Traveler, he saw a small group of Union officers riding down the hill, preceded by the white flag of truce. At first, Lee did not recognize the man in the slouch hat who was on Meade's left and slightly ahead of Meade. Walter Taylor exclaimed, "General, that's Grant with Meade!"

Men of the South and of the North who, minutes before, had been struggling to kill one another, now stood in quiet awe and respect as the two legends of the war rode out to meet.

A subdued feeling of exultation swept through the boys in blue, while remorse and anxiety began to build among the boys of Lee's army. But most in one way or another were relieved to know that the killing of Americans by Americans was coming to an end.

Grant and Lee, after exchanging greetings, proceeded in silence to the tent that had been hastily erected a mile or so from the battlefield.

Neither spoke as they dismounted and entered the tent, where Grant gestured to a seat for Lee, and then sat across from him. Orderlies were giving them steaming mugs of coffee, even though the temperature was in the high seventies, when in came Meade, Longstreet, and Meade's chief of staff, Brigadier General Humphreys. Walter Taylor also arrived and took his usual place near Lee.

Reaching inside his coat, Grant produced two cigars, one of which he offered Lee, who politely refused. Grant stuck one of the cigars back into his coat pocket, and then began to speak, holding the other cigar in his hand.

"General Lee, although you and I both served in the Mexican War, we never met, to the best of my recollection." Lee nodded in agreement.

After a moment's pause, Grant drew a paper from his other coat pocket. Unfolding it, he handed it to Lee. As Lee studied the paper, the silence was broken by the entry of Stuart and Fitz Lee, both appearing distressed. It was Fitz Lee who responded to Lee's inquiring look.

"Sir, it's Rooney. He has been wounded and is unconscious. The doctors are treating him now. We thought you should know in case you wanted to see him …."

Meade leaned over to Grant and whispered that Rooney was one of Lee's sons, and that he commanded a cavalry brigade.

There was an awkward pause as Fitz tried to say the right words, but it was apparent that he thought Lee's son might be dying.

Grant stood up and went around the table to Lee. Placing his hand gently on Lee's arm, Grant softly spoke, "General, we can continue this tomorrow. If any medical assistance is needed, please so inform us."

Lee arose, the burden he carried visible in the set of his features. "Thank you, General. I shall meet with you tomorrow morning at such time as you wish. I will confer with my corps commanders to inform them of your generous terms and of my decision to accept them." Lee paused. Then, in a clearly reluctant manner, he said that his men had been without proper rations for more than two days, and any spare rations would be gratefully accepted. Grant nodded, and later that day, 25,000 rations were sent to the Confederates, a gesture that did much to aid the beginning of reconciliation between the South and North.

Stuart and Fitz Lee exchanged a quick glance, then Stuart spoke. "Sir, there is some additional news you should know. Hill was mortally wounded and died just as we were departing to come here."

Lee's head bowed, seconds passed, then he raised his head and looked at Stuart. "As of now, you have command of Third Corps," and turning to Fitz Lee, "and you have command of the cavalry."

Lee shook hands with Grant, and departed, followed by Stuart and Fitz Lee. A mix of blue and gray were retrieving the wounded and burying the dead. They stopped and saluted as Lee rode by.

JULY 10, 1863

The dawn revealed a cloudless sky, promising a beautiful day, but it was anything but beautiful for General Robert E. Lee. He had visited the tent where his son Rooney was showing a slight improvement, enough to give Lee hope that his son would eventually regain his full health. Now he was headed for the meeting that he dreaded, his head bowed as he rode. After so many victories at the cost of so many lives, it had come to this.

The sound of a sharp command followed by the rattle of muskets being brought to Shoulder Arms broke his musing, and raising his head to an erect posture, he raised his right arm in a return salute to the Union troops who lined the way ahead.

Grant stood outside the tent and greeted Lee as he dismounted.

"Good morning, General."

Lee could not bring himself to agree and merely nodded in reply.

Entering the tent, Lee and Grant took seats on either side of the small table which some enterprising staffer had covered with a green baize cloth. Each was then handed a copy of the terms of surrender, which each signed after a careful reading, The copies were exchanged and signed, and the Army of Northern Virginia was officially the prisoner of the Army of the Potomac.

Lee handed Taylor his copy, and stood up, speaking for the first time since his arrival.

"General Grant, I want you to know that I, as well as the men in the rank and file, deeply appreciate the generous terms you have given and the kind acts of so many of your officers and men. I will do all I can to assist in healing the scars of war and in restoring the union of our separated states into the United States of America."

* * *

After returning to his army, Lee wrote his farewell to the Army of Northern Virginia:

"After arduous service marked by unsurpassed courage and fortitude, the Army of Northern Virginia has been compelled to yield to overwhelming numbers and resources.

"I need not tell the brave survivors of so many hard-fought battles, who have remained steadfast to the last, that I have consented to this result from no distrust of them but feeling that valor and devotion could accomplish nothing that could compensate for the loss that must have attended the continuance of the contest, I determined to avoid the useless sacrifice of those whose past services have endeared them to their countrymen.

"By the terms of the agreement, officers and men can return to their homes and remain until exchanged. You will take with you the satisfaction that proceeds from the consciousness of duty faithfully performed; and I earnestly pray that a Merciful God will extend to you His blessing and protection.

> "With an unceasing admiration of your constancy and devotion to your Country, and a grateful remembrance of your kind and generous consideration for myself, I bid you all an affectionate farewell."
> /S/ R. E. Lee

That afternoon, accompanied by his son whose wagon was guarded by a contingent of US cavalry headed by Captain Norris, Lee mounted Traveler and rode off to take his place in history.

* * *

General Robert E. Lee, CSA
David John Murphy

EPILOGUE

Although President Jefferson Davis immediately moved the capital of the Confederacy to Atlanta with the intent of carrying on from there, it was obvious to General Joseph E. Johnston that the cause of Southern freedom was a lost cause. He surrendered the Army of Tennessee to Sherman within a week of Lee's surrender. Kirby Smith followed with the capitulation of forces west of the Mississippi. The war had ended for all.

Jefferson Davis eluded capture for over a month, but finally was taken prisoner as he tried to slip aboard a ship departing Wilmington, North Carolina, bound for Cuba.

President Lincoln oversaw the reconstruction of the South with compassion and generosity, winning the support of many Southerners. At the end of his second term, he retired to a farm near Springfield, Illinois. His soft treatment of the South during the occupation and reconstruction period alienated the Radical branch of the Republicans, causing them to oppose Lincoln's initiatives to revive the Southern economy. Lincoln died from a stroke in 1874, revered by the veterans of his army.

Grant retired from the Army in 1869 and considered going into politics, but was dissuaded from doing so by Sherman, whose brother, a U. S. senator, had revealed to Sherman the devious practices and cut-throat world of the politicians.

Grant strongly recommended a full pardon for Lee, but due to the opposition in Congress by the Radical branch of the Republican party, Lincoln could not comply with Grant's recommendation. Lee lost his Arlington estate and lived in civic limbo. He accepted the offer to be president of Washington College, in Lexington, Virginia, where he succumbed to a heart attack in 1870.

Upwards of 300,000 Americans, North and South combined, were lost, most to disease (The actual losses from 1861 to the end of the war in 1865 amounted to over 600,000.) Despite the destruction, the loss of property, the loss of so many lives, and the enduring pain of so many from both physical and mental wounds, despite all these, the young country survived and prospered. But the indelible effect on the nation will forever remain.

Harper's Ferry
iStock.com

AUTHOR'S NOTES

Although I have tried to follow actual history where possible, I remind the reader that this is a work of fiction. However, in developing the plot, I endeavored to stay as close to reality as my talents, or lack thereof, would allow. In this regard, it resembles a war game.

When I began, I truly did not know whether Meade could have so crippled the Army of Northern Virginia as to render it no longer able to function. But as the story unfolded, it became evident that if the powers that were in the North, Lincoln, Stanton, Halleck, and yes, Meade, had vigorously used all the forces available to them and without delay, Lee could have been trapped as occurred in this book.

Critical to Union success was near immediate interdiction of Lee's logistics.

There are undoubtedly literally hundreds of scenarios that could have been played, but in view of the endless controversy regarding Lincoln's opinion that Meade could have bloodied Lee's army so badly that Lee would have been forced to surrender, I chose to make that issue the core of the story.

The idea for writing this "what if" novel was the result of reading the trilogy of Gettysburg by Newt Gingrich and William Forstchen that was so well done. In considering their description of what might have been, I wondered why Meade and Halleck had failed to quickly interdict Lee's line of supply from Winchester, it being such an obvious vulnerability for Lee. And the story grew from there.

Throughout the story, I have tried to portray the heavy weight of responsibility borne by a senior commander in combat whose decisions result either in victory or defeat, and whose orders can determine life or death for his people. Adding the inevitable fog of war and the occurrence of unforeseen circumstances can make command in combat an almost unbearable load to carry. Yet the average citizen is unaware of this, and historians give it little heed, if at all.

Lee's Farewell words are his exact words delivered at Appomattox, with the number of years adjusted.

A bundle of thanks is due to my favorite illustrator, David John Murphy, whose artwork so aptly and beautifully enhances this novel, artwork well worth acquiring.

My thanks also to my publisher, BSP. The motivation generated by Rob Kosberg's lectures, combined with the ready assistance of May Cheng, Meghan McDonald and Steve Fata has made what could have been an onerous chore into a pleasant learning experience. This, combined with Rob Kosberg's invaluable and inspiring lectures, show me that Best Seller Publishing is an outstanding asset for us self-publishers.

I hope the reader enjoys the book. Any facts of history that are misstated and anything found to be implausible are all my responsibility. In describing the character and actions of actual persons I have portrayed them as history has recorded them.

Questions and discussion done in a reasonable way are most welcome. The Civil War is the genesis of many of the issues confronting us today, and the more each of us learns and understands about the War, the better will be the political health of our beloved nation

POSTSCRIPT

The failures in leadership and generalship of the first three commanders of the Union Army of the Potomac deprived that army of any meaningful successes in the field until Gettysburg, with the possible exception of Antietam/Sharpsburg.

Lee was the victor in the Seven Days campaign that drove McClellan from the approaches to Richmond, at Fredericksburg where the Union army suffered heavy losses under Burnside, and at Chancellorsville when Hooker lost his confidence and allowed Lee to win on the gamble maneuver of Jackson's corps. Lee should have been defeated at Antietam, but McClellan's refusal to use Porter's corps, together with Burnside's inept handling of his corps, allowed Lee to escape with a draw.

The men of the Army of the Potomac deserved better leadership, and once they finally received it, they showed that they could fight just as well as any other Americans.

Made in the USA
Coppell, TX
17 March 2022